ANGEL IN DEMISE

MYSTIC'S END MYSTERIES BOOK 2

LEANNE LEEDS

BADCHEN PUBLISHING

Angel in Demise
Published by Badchen Publishing
4500 Williams Dr., Suite 212-269
Georgetown, TX 78633 USA

ANGEL IN DEMISE

ONE

"It looks like a fancy cage for chickens. *Really* small chickens," Spike said as I flexed the wire for the angel's arm. Settling back and studying the frame, I rescanned the sketch of the angel statue on the desk next to me. "If someone crashes into that thing, won't it just get all bent out of shape?"

"You're getting me bent out of shape," I murmured as I twirled my hand to adjust the armature. It flickered briefly and suddenly straightened itself. "There. I think that looks better."

"It looks nothing like your sketch, though," Spike said as he hovered over the desk.

"That's because this is just the frame. It will."

"Of course it will," Martin Salvi called from the front of the store.

I sighed, cursing myself for not remembering to lock the front door behind me after I went to get the mail.

"Back here, Martin," I called in a chipper tone. Well, as chipper a tone I could muster considering the elegant, handsome entertainment complex manager hadn't called before he came over.

I was in the middle of a project and already behind schedule. I hated to be interrupted.

To be honest, it shouldn't have surprised me. Martin Salvi never called anymore. He realized if he called I would push off seeing him, and Mr. Rich and Handsome really didn't appreciate that at all.

"Is that the angel for Hugh's party?" Martin asked as he strolled in, sat down, and placed a large brown bag on one of the craft tables without waiting for an invitation. He began unpacking plastic containers of what I presumed was food—judging by the incredible smells that accompanied him.

My stomach rumbled audibly.

"Yeah, but I'm a little behind," I frowned. "I didn't know you knew Hubert Maddox."

"Everybody knows Hugh and Della."

"Let me guess," I replied wryly. "They own greyhounds."

"Nope," Martin said with a grin. "They do bet on them, though. They have a luxury box at the track and come fairly often."

"Of course they do," I murmured as Martin tossed a scrap of steak to Gideon, my pet greyhound. Gideon raced to seize the flying meat, but it ricocheted off the area between his eyes and onto the floor. The greyhound scrambled wildly to snag it. "What brings you here, Martin?"

"You, as always," Martin said, his smooth face bursting into a wide smile that could be classified as genuine or manipulative, depending what you thought of Martin Salvi. And I hadn't determined yet what I thought of Martin Salvi.

I looked at him, my face stoic.

"You are a hard nut to crack, madame, I will give you that," Martin admitted as he leaned back on the stool and chuckled. "My determination will get through that hard outer shell you have, though, I guarantee you." He examined the table and grabbed a container. "Shrimp scampi?" he asked, holding it up.

I narrowed my eyes. "You're starting to know my favorites."

"Well, of course I am. We're friends, aren't we?" he suggested, his eyes glistening.

I didn't respond as I grabbed the container from him and opened up the shrimp scampi. I might not be sure how I felt about Martin, but I *was* secure in my feelings about the food he brought to try and woo me. I delved into its buttery garlic goodness.

"Do you think you'll have it done in time?" Martin inquired, waving toward the angel armature.

"I *have* to," I confessed with my mouth full, shrugging. "They paid extra to make certain it was ready to go for their garden party. A lot more, actually. Mrs. Maddox was emphatic about it. She was emphatic about quite a lot of things, actually."

"Della? That's surprising. She's such a laid-back woman."

"She didn't seem laid back to me. *Usually* a garden statue would be shaped out of marble or cast in bronze or something that can stand up to the elements," I pointed out as I speared a shrimp. "She was insistent that it be done out of plaster of Paris, and that it not be cast. She preferred it carved. At the size she needs, it's a little tricky."

"You do an awful lot here," Martin said seriously, the gleam still in his eye. "You take commissions, teach classes, sell art. A little bird told me you even teach once a week at the nursing home without charging them. True?"

"True. I didn't realize little birds were talking about me so much," I frowned as I finished the last of my scampi and slid off the stool to rinse the plastic box so I could place it in the recycling.

"Did I say something wrong?" Martin asked.

I had already been through one situation with Gabriel Wilcox spilling things I would have rather people not gossiped about. I wasn't happy to hear I was still a topic of conversation in the town. "Next time you want to know something about me? Ask me."

"People always talk when I ask questions, but not you. It's actually difficult for me to get people to stop talking around me," he laughed. Then, Martin grew serious as he scratched his chin and considered me. "Perhaps that's why I find you so compelling, Fortuna. I ask questions and yet I never seem to get answers."

"I answer you. You find me fascinating because it's incomprehensible to you that there's something you want that you can't have," I told him as I raised my eyebrow. He laughed.

"It's true. There's been nothing I wanted that I didn't get, eventually." He gave me his best smolderingly sexy look. I rolled my eyes.

"I'll put it in my will that you get my ashes when I die. See? Always a solution that gets everyone what they want."

Martin laughed at me again as Gideon barked.

* * *

It had been three months since I left the Magical Midway and moved to Mystic's End.

In that time, an old woman slapped me and declared me the official mystic of the town (even though I still did not understand what that meant). The most influential man in town had pursued me relentlessly (though he often brought delicious food, so I'll concede I didn't demand he stop with much—okay, any—vigor). And a skeleton in my bedroom turned into a ghostly roommate.

Oh, and I was still no closer to finding out which one of these townspeople I was related to, much less why someone left me on the steps of the old police station/courthouse in the center of the town square years ago.

The town square my shop was located in.

You would think the fact that I was a witch would make unwinding some of these situations easier, but nope. Before moving here, I had committed to a set of ethics regarding my telepathic powers, and I was proud of myself that I kept to them—despite feeling the periodic urge to rummage through everyone's head for answers. If you scream it out psychically, I'll listen, but I *don't* go brain-diving without permission.

Those ethics, though, didn't make any of the things I was doing any easier.

Mystic Moon Gallery, despite all this, was doing great. I did a brisk trade in art supplies and classes, and a few tourists even dropped by to purchase paintings, pottery and sculpture done by the locals.

"You need to just go out with that guy," Spike, the ghost that haunted my store/apartment, announced as he glided back in from the front of the shop. "He's handsome, he's rich, and he's *definitely* into you."

"First, when someone courts you with gourmet food, you take your time deciding," I told the incorporeal punk as his huge mohawk passed through the light fixture. "Once you decide, the gourmet gravy train could dry up. Not that I would expect a ghost to know that since, you know, you can't eat."

Spike gasped. "Are you just using him for his food?"

"Did *I* invite *him* over?" I asked Spike. "I've told him no multiple times. If *he* wants to incorporate bribery into our friendship, who am I to say no to Beef Wellington?"

"Feeling a *little* sassy tonight, are we?" Spike said as he turned around, crossed his arms, and gave me a judge-y look.

"I am impressed that you refrained from using the b-word."

"Yeah, well, my extensive four-letter-word repertoire doesn't have the same jolt as it used to since you and Gideon are the only two that hear it, and you just get mad at me," he informed me while pouting.

"You're dead. Use the afterlife to learn how to sound like something other than a trucker."

"You mean like *Martin Salvi?*" Spike sing-songed, mimicking an exaggerated elegance. I glowered at him. Then he made disgusting kissing noises as he wrapped his own arms around his torso. "Or *Gabriel Wilcox?*" More juvenile kissing noises.

I inspected my crystal ball and wondered whether I could solidify Spike enough with a spell to hit him in the head with it.

"Just because you can't get yourself out of this building long enough to meet other ghosts doesn't mean that you get to keep a running commentary on my private life for sport, Spike," I warned him, raising my hand. "Maybe I can't dislodge you, but I can make it so I don't have to hear you."

Spike froze and his face fell. Gideon whined, his tail drooping.

Great. Now I felt bad.

I sighed. "Dude, just grow up a little, okay?

This isn't high school. I don't need to be ridiculed about Martin or Gabriel. It's not funny."

"But I was just having a little fun," Spike told me sullenly. Looking up, he grudgingly apologized. I nodded. "You're the *only* entertainment I have in here besides the pup," he lamented.

"Read a book," I quipped.

Spike flew over to the bookshelf and jammed his hands into the shelves repeatedly. He gawked at me as they passed through the volumes as if they weren't even there.

I sighed again. "Okay, why don't you and I find some shows you want to watch, and I can rig up something so Gideon can start and stop them for you on the television."

The ghost paused and stared at me. "Really?" he blinked, shocked.

"If we can teach the dog to do it, yeah," I nodded.

"You'd do that for me?" Spike was so touched by my suggestion that my heart broke for him. Even though his house was now filled with people, he was still so lonely.

"If it'll get you to stop making kissing noises like you're a ten-year-old on a playground, you betcha."

Gideon barked and wagged his tail.

* * *

"There. Done," I said two days later as Gideon looked on. "What do you think, Gideon? You think they will like the statue?"

Gideon barked.

I had accomplished most of it the old-fashioned way, but when I lost a half a day to rigging up a television system for dog paws—and then another day teaching the dog how to turn on the television and start shows for Spike—I wound up having to cheat a little to make the deadline.

"That is *charming*, Fortuna," Azalea Cotton, a seventeen-year-old aspiring artist, said as she peeked out from behind her canvas. Her pixie like features showed off the spot of red acrylic smeared on her nose. "It's so *lifelike*. But how come there's no foundation? I mean, that thin wood won't hold it, will it?"

"They already have a pedestal for it, or so I'm told," I revealed, thrilled that she spotted what was missing. "Someone should be by in about an hour to move it to the Maddoxes' garden and install it."

"I *love* the spear," Azalea breathed, and suddenly she turned behind her to grab her sketch book. Staring at the angel, she started frantically sketching it. Then she hesitated and looked up. "I'm sorry, do you mind?"

"Not at all, sketch away," I told her as I glanced

at the clock. "Quickly, though, the movers are coming at three or so."

"No problem," she said as she bit her lip and looked down, her intense eyes darting back up every so often.

"Fortuna!" someone called from the front of the store.

"I'll be right back, Azalea," I told the girl as I trudged through the studio and into the storefront. Joe Bradley, a quiet young man in his mid-twenties, stood by the counter. "Hey, Joe, what do you need?"

"Hi, um, I need more acrylic paint," he held up a tube, "and a fan brush. Actually, make it two. My cat decided my current one would make a great cat toy," he grinned sheepishly.

"Oh, no! I hope she didn't eat much of the paint," I told him as I leaned down and snagged two of his favorite brand's fan brushes out of the drawer.

"Let's just say Mars Black is impressive looking on a white Persian, though I doubt I'll be using her as a canvas anytime soon," he said. We both chuckled as I handed him the brushes.

He dropped the money into my hand and I rang him up. I offered him a bag, but he shook his head and dropped the items into his backpack. "Thanks, Fortuna. It's nice to be able to run down to a shop now instead of waiting days for a delivery."

"Anytime," I nodded and grinned, waiting for

him to leave.

The quiet young man did not leave. He fidgeted, and then fidgeted some more, and then took a deep breath. "So, um, Fortuna, I was wondering if—"

"Fortuna!" Azalea yelled from the back. "There's someone banging on your back door! Should I open it?"

"Just a second, Azalea! I'll get it," I hollered back through the archway. Turning back, I leaned toward the quiet young man. "Sorry, Joe, what was it?"

"Ah, so...nothing. Never mind," he answered as he peered down toward his shoes and stepped backwards. Raising his hand up, he gave a half wave and shyly met my eyes. "You're busy, I'll go."

"Are you sure?" I asked, concerned. "If you need something else—"

"No, it's good, I'm fine," he said as he reared back into a card stand. "Oh, crap, man, I'm sorry!" Joe said as he burned red, reaching out to steady it.

"I want pictures of your cat with the paint on him!" I told him, ignoring his awkward collision.

"Yeah, okay, sure," Joe said, and he turned and headed out the door.

"Fortuna!" Azalea yelled louder.

"I'm coming! I'm coming!" I hollered again as I twisted around and headed toward the back.

TWO

"He's a complete buffoon, that's what *he* is," Pepper Stanford fumed as she stomped around the studio kicking chairs just enough that they made a racket, but not enough to do any real damage.

"Who?" I asked as I trailed behind her and quietly slid the chairs back into their places.

"My boss, stupid Elroy Conroe, the editor of the stupid *Mystic's End Herald*," she sputtered bitterly. Pepper looked like a spoiled child that had just been informed she couldn't go to a party, her lower lip sticking out to finish her perfectly injured expression. "I asked to investigate the Abernathys' business investments and do you know what he assigned me instead? Do you *know*?"

"No, but I bet dollars to donuts you're about to tell me," I said sarcastically, and her lip jutted out even further. Azalea was quietly packing her paint brushes, eyes wide.

"That idiot assigned me to cover the Maddox garden party. A *garden* party! What's investigative about *that*?"

"I don't think he meant it to be an investigative assignment, Pepper," I told her, nodding to Azalea as she scurried out of the room. "It sounds like it's just an assignment like any other assignment."

"Yes, yes, exactly! How could he *do* that? He assured me—*promised* me—that I would start getting meatier stories, and then he sticks me on a *garden party society report*," she fumed, flinging herself down on a stool in front of Azalea's painting. Her eyes snapped open, and she looked the canvas up and down. "Wow, this is incredible," she said, her attitude completely transforming. "That girl did this?"

Pepper Stanford was exhausting.

To call the woman high-spirited would be generous—mercurial was more like it. Impetuous and bold, Pepper *could* be a determined force of nature when she fixated on something significant.

When she obsessed over something *unimportant*, though, she could be intensely annoying.

"Yes, that's Azalea's painting," I told her as I took the wet canvas off the easel and carried it out of Pepper's potential path of destruction. "Look, you knew that Mr. Conroe wasn't going to turn the *Herald* into the *New York Times* overnight, assigning you explosive story after explosive story," I pointed out, turning back to her. "Why are you taking this so hard?"

"Because he promised he would assign me more stories that had some *meat* to them," she pouted again, crossing her arms. "A society garden party? That happens every year? I could just take out the story I wrote last year, change the order of the words, hand it in and I doubt *anyone* would notice."

"*You* would notice," I told her firmly.

"Ugh, stop being all reasonable," Pepper glared at me. "I want you to *share* in my indignation, not talk me down off a ledge."

"Wait—*what* ledge?"

"The ledge where I quit my job and blog full time about stories that *matter*," Pepper said a sigh. "I'm *wasted* at this stupid paper, Fortuna. Maybe I can get some advertising and make enough to survive, do the things I want to do. I don't get anything out of this—"

"You get press credentials and a paycheck," I pointed out as I leaned against the wall. "Those two things have to be worth something. Maybe even writing about the odd garden party?"

"It's not even *writing* about the party that bugs me," she said. "It's the *going* to the party that bugs me. I can't stand those rich people—they're everything that's wrong with this town, all on one canapé-gorged deck. I could write the stupid profile of it in my sleep. I just don't want to *go*. It's a *waste* of time."

"Well, then you're in luck, because I've been invited," I told her, smirking. She gawked at me, her jaw dropping. "Oh, close your mouth. This statue is going to be displayed at their party, and since I did it, they extended an invitation to me so I could see its final installation. I'm not joining the bourgeoisie or anything."

"Well, at least I could write about *that* and help you out a bit, get you some press," Pepper said as she turned and looked at the statue. "Not going with Martin, I take it?"

"Wasn't asked."

"Or Gabriel?"

"I don't know if he's going," I told her, watching her back carefully for any sign the idea bothered her.

Detective Gabriel Wilcox was the first person I met in Mystic's End after the real estate agent. Our friendship began when he stopped by to accuse me of being a con artist psychic.

Okay, maybe not *right* then.

Pepper and Gabriel had been a couple for several years, a relationship that was hard for me to picture. Pepper was as fiery as Gabriel was even-tempered. Opposites may have attracted, but they didn't work when trying to build a long-term relationship.

"Oh, he'll go, doubtless with Miss Bessie," Pepper told me as she turned back toward me. "Claire doesn't escort her to those types of things, and she inv*ariably* goes."

"Well, then *you* can be my date," I told her cheerfully.

She raised her eyebrow. "Giving the other team a shot? Because I have to tell you, I *know* which team I play for, and it's the one—"

"No, no, not a *date* date," I explained to her, rolling my eyes. "I'd rather not go alone, if you want to know the truth."

"Oh, fine, then. Pick you up at eight?" she asked.

"Sounds good."

* * *

"Wow, this is incredible," I breathed as Pepper and I strolled into the candlelit hallway of an enormous mansion. A butler bowed and reached out his arm toward a large room soaked in a golden glow while another small woman in a maid's uniform held out a tray of champagne. Pepper and I both seized a glass.

"Hugh and Della are *old* money," Pepper said softly as we picked our way through the regally-dressed crowd. "Well, Hugh is. Della married into old money when she snagged Hugh."

"What does he do for a living?" I asked as we stepped out onto the patio through wide-open double glass doors.

"Spend Daddy's money," she responded as she nodded to this person and that person. Some attendees pointedly avoided her. "They just love when the proletariat drink their fancy wine, don't they?"

"Are you a Marxist?" I whispered to her.

"No, but just for your information, if I was, I would consider you to be *petite bourgeois*."

"Good to know," I told her, having no idea what she was talking about.

"He was a journalist, you know," she said as we made our way toward the end of the patio where, I guessed, the statue sat under the large canvas I could see.

"Who?"

"Karl Marx," she answered.

"Um. Okay," I acknowledged.

"Didn't you study world history like, ever?"

"I went to a boarding school," I told her.

"Ugh, how bougie." Pepper rolled her eyes.

"You *are* a Marxist," I murmured.

"Get stomped on by the wealthy and influential a few times, Fortuna, and you might recognize it as a compelling political leaning," she advised me as we settled on a place by the rail to stand. "But no, I'm not a Marxist. I just read a lot."

"Ms. Delphi!" Hugh Maddox boomed with his arms expanded, a champagne glass in each hand. The host of the party was dressed in a loud blue suit, a huge blue orchid boutonniere pinned to his breast. "Della and I are so pleased that you could make our little soiree! The angel was splendid, *perfect*! And who's your little—oh, it's *you*," Mr. Maddox's tone turned icy as he spotted Pepper Stanford. "Who let *you* in?" he demanded.

"Press pass, Mr. Maddox," Pepper said gleefully as she hoisted her badge. "I'm writing up the review of this little shindig for the paper, so unless you want me to point out your sour disposition, be a *little* nicer to me. Or just don't talk to me," she shrugged. "That'll work, too."

"It wasn't sour until I saw *you* were in

attendance, dear," the millionaire answered haughtily. Turning his back on Pepper, the man grinned broadly at me again. "You will be *so* pleased to see what we've done with your statue, dear. Della has the whole thing covered in the most lovely lights! You'll be so pleased, I'm sure."

I looked over at the tarpaulin and could see wires snaking out from underneath.

"I'm sure it will be lovely, Mr. Maddox," I told him.

"The silver color is just lovely," he said as he turned away. I frowned.

"Silver?" I called, but he kept walking. Turning to Pepper, I remarked that there was no silver on the statue. She shrugged.

"Maybe they added something for the lights or something?"

That would turn out to be the understatement of the year.

* * *

"I had this produced, this angel, in remembrance of my father, Tiberius Maddox," Hugh Maddox told the hushed crowd clustered around the rustling canvas. "My brother and I could think of no better reminder of our father than the magnificent angel that pointed him toward heaven just two months ago."

"Yeah, like *that's* likely," Pepper snorted in my ear. "Tib Maddox was a lech, a swindler, and a cheat."

"Shhhhh!" a woman dripping in diamonds hissed at Pepper, who rolled her eyes in return.

"We contracted this beautiful, custom-made statue from the Mystic Moon Gallery," Hugh boomed as he pointed toward me. "My wife worked with Fortuna Delphi on the specs, and though Ms. Delphi made a few modifications of her own and Della was a little put out, I think the silver is *excellent*."

"What changes?" I murmured. "I didn't alter it at all. It's precisely what she asked me for."

Climbing up on the ledge behind the sculpture, a fountain behind him, Hugh Maddox pulled the tarp up and over the angel with a passionate flourish. "Alfred, if you please?" he called toward his battalion of butlers standing off to the right.

My initial thought was that I would kill whoever dumped metallic silver paint all over my gorgeous, white statue. The color wasn't even well applied, and it gobbed in pools on the crevices I had so laboriously chiseled out.

Or, okay, cast a spell to chisel out.

It was still work.

My second thought was that the lights that came on were dreadful. In two seconds, the air grew warm from spotlights and string lights and flickering lights, and the courtyard looked like a Christmas party despite it being the heart of spring.

My third thought was that I picked up a buzz.

And it wasn't the buzz of an awed crowd.

Hugh Maddox reached out proudly to put his hand on the shoulder of the piece, and a sizzling zapping noise replaced the low level buzz in my ear. His face turned to shock and his limbs jerked with tension as he clutched his chest.

"What's happening?" someone from the crowd demanded, mystified.

"The angel! It's the angel! It's killing him!" another cried.

"He has a pacemaker! Turn the damn lights off!"

Della looked at her spouse, her face unreadable.

As the butlers scrambled to turn off the lights, darkness settled on the patio and the sound of crackling ceased. For a second or two, nobody moved.

Then Hugh Maddox fell backward into the fountain.

Dead.

* * *

"Try not to look like a dog that just got thrown a bone, will you?" I whispered at Pepper.

"Oh, come on, can't you just see the title? Killed by an Angel," she informed me, glancing up from a steno pad she was rapidly writing in. "Daddy's Electric Angel. The Maddox Party: It was Electric," she said with positively no compassion for the deceased man being hauled, wet, out of the fountain by paramedics.

"Maybe he's not dead," I told her as I watched them work on him.

"He's dead, or those are the slowest paramedics in history."

"You're *really* awful, you know that?" I said to her, horrified. She shrugged.

I bit my lip as the paramedics respectfully put the canvas Hugh Maddox had dragged off the angel over him. One spoke softly into a cell phone while the other ensured all parts of Hugh's lifeless body were concealed.

Della Maddox wailed as she stared at her departed partner, held by some man I didn't know. Another man, stricken, stood beside her, being talked to by a younger, awkward looking young man. The butlers and maids looked frightened and confused, as if uncertain of what to do.

"What on earth happened?" Gabriel Wilcox asked as he and Miss Bessie shuffled up to us slowly. "We were inside getting Gram some food when people started screaming."

"Looked to me like Fortuna's statue electrocuted Maddox," Pepper told him as she waved her pencil in the body's direction. "He put his hand on it. It started buzzing when they lit it up, he grabbed it, froze, and then fell over dead when they turned the lights off."

Gabriel glanced at me, dumbfounded. "Did you have an electrician hook the lights up or do it yourself?"

"I didn't hook any lights up!" I insisted. "I just carved a sculpture, that's it. No lights, and no ugly silver paint, either."

"Well, he didn't touch the cables or wires," Martin Salvi said as he strolled up and joined us. Gabriel frowned at him. "I was standing behind him when he reached out for the statue. He put his hand on the shoulder."

"Who invited *you* here?" Miss Bessie barked at him as she shoved her glasses up higher on her nose. "Shoo. This is a private conversation."

"Miss Bessie, marvelous to see you," Martin nodded, ignoring her demand. "Gabriel," he added with a little less enthusiasm.

"Gabe, you need to get her out of here," Miss Bessie poked Gabriel and signaled toward me. "Before your boss shows up."

"Why?" I asked, perplexed.

"They'll need *someone* to blame," she informed me. "You did the sculpture."

"You may want to grab a ride with Gabe, actually," Pepper told me distractedly as her eyes scanned every inch of the scene. "I will be here a while."

"I can take her," Martin stepped forward.

"No, I've got her," Gabriel insisted as he reached out for me.

"Not to be insulting, Detective Wilcox, but that's a crime scene, and you're a police officer," Martin said with a hand raised, his eyes narrowing as he stared at Gabe. "I don't think Ms. Delphi should be around you at the moment. Not without a lawyer."

"Oh, for heavens'—" Miss Bessie declared, but Pepper cut her off.

"Actually, he's right," she announced as she looked at Gabriel. "I realize that the two of you are friends, but that man just died after handling a statue she made. He died in front of over a hundred witnesses, and you don't know who will catch the case."

Gabriel's face twisted in frustration as he looked back and forth between Pepper and Martin.

"Look, you want to protect her, Gabe?" Pepper asked him. "Let Money-bucks over here take her home. That's the best thing you can do right now. Stay away from her until you know how this is going to play. Maybe we'll get lucky and it will be ignored like every other crime in this town."

"Crime?" I asked, and gulped.

"Now that that's settled, are you ready?" Martin asked, and he gently placed his arm around me. "My limo is just outside the front door."

"Of *course* it is," Pepper snorted. Martin smiled pleasantly at her.

"If you're sure," I told her, glancing back at the scene.

"Go," Pepper pointed toward the house.

I went. Glancing back once, I saw Gabriel and Miss Bessie watching me while Pepper stared at the statue, her face intent on unraveling its secret.

THREE

"Straight home?" Martin asked after we settled into the cavernous limousine. The privacy panel cracked ever so slightly, but I couldn't see the driver.

"I'm sorry?" I asked Martin distractedly as I gazed back toward the Maddox mansion. A gurney rolled out toward an ambulance parked next to the limo. Just behind the ambulance, Chief Clutterbuck walked side by side with Bobby Newsom.

"Did you want to go straight home, or could I interest you in some dinner?" Martin asked again. "I didn't see you earlier at the party, so I wondered if you had anything to eat. Or if you might be hungry."

The limo lurched away from the scene, and I turned back toward Martin.

He really was handsome.

A little over six feet, he was tall but not too tall. Dark brown eyes and hair, a conservative jacket and tie—he just seemed elegantly matched. His expression was always tinged with a bemused air, as if everything he came across made him just slightly amused.

"Did I say something wrong?" he smiled politely after my staring went on just one second too long.

"No, Martin, no. I'm sorry, I didn't mean to stare," I blushed and turned back toward the front of the car. "I'm just...a man just *died*. I'm a *little* rattled."

"Yes, but are you *hungry*?" he asked for the third time as he leaned toward me. I looked back and found his bemused expression unshaken by the night's deadly events. "And for the record, you may stare at me as much as you wish."

"I swear, you people are like the Stepford citizens. You and Pepper, both of you, just completely unrattled by Hugh Maddox dropping dead right in front of you," I snapped. "Don't you care *at all*?"

"Fortuna, people die," Martin said with a shrug. "Hugh Maddox was not a friend, he was a customer. While I feel sorry for the man, and it's a shame that he passed on, I'm not emotionally broken up about it, no. Honestly," he said tilting his head. "I'm a little surprised that you are."

I didn't answer him, but finally, I exhaled.

"I'm sorry," I told him, looking up hesitantly. "It was uncalled for, jumping on you like that. I think I'm freaked out about the angel. It's just...something I created killed someone."

"I *highly* doubt that," Martin frowned. "You said yourself that you didn't put any of the lights on it and besides, the man had a pacemaker, Fortuna. At least if the crowd is to be believed. Maybe he simply had a heart attack from the excitement of the evening."

"And the buzzing sound?" I asked in a tone that sounded suspiciously close to sarcasm.

"Could have been anything. His father passed away after a long, painful illness no more than two months ago. The man has clearly been through a difficult time and judging by his size? I wouldn't guess that he was the healthiest of men on his best day."

"Maybe you're right," I agreed reluctantly. "I still think something happened out there, though."

"You're right, something happened. A man passed away after a stressful year, the culmination of an unhealthy life," Martin declared emphatically, his tone leaving no room for debate. "I insist that you let me take your mind off this tragedy. You'll feel better when you get something to eat."

"It's not a date," I warned him.

"What *is* a date, really?" Martin smiled as he called up to his driver to take us into Little Rock for the evening.

* * *

I popped another wood-roasted mushroom in my mouth and breathed in the spring air. We sat on the patio of Yoko's, a European-bistro styled restaurant, overlooking the Arkansas River.

"These are superb," I told Martin. "And the place is fantastic. What a view."

"I knew you had good taste," Martin smiled as he casually raised his arm and glanced at the waiter. Without being told anything, the waiter returned with the carafe of house wine and refilled our glasses. Martin nodded without looking at the man, and he withdrew.

"Oh, really? How did you know that?"

"You have an artist's palate," Martin said, his voice lowering as he leaned forward and rested his hands on the table. "For art, for food...perhaps even for men. Elegant and refined."

I put my elbow on the table and chewed my

food slightly open-mouthed. He chuckled and raised an eyebrow.

"Are you determined to be the opposite of what you're expected to be? That rebellious artistic spirit, I take it?"

"There's nothing *rebellious* about my artistic spirit," I told him as I reached for my glass of wine. "You just think you have me pegged, that's all. And I don't think you do."

"No?"

"No. I ran from this when I was younger," I told him, opening up a little for the first time since he began to pursue me. I don't know if it was the atmosphere, the wine, or the death I had witnessed. Maybe it was all three. But I let him get a foot in the door. "Money, elegant manners, all of this garbage that people aspire to. It's meaningless if you're not happy."

"You're not happy?"

"I wasn't happy," I admitted and looked away, the burning intensity in his eyes making me slightly uncomfortable. "My childhood was filled with boarding schools, and yachts, and fancy cotillions, and I hated every minute."

"Why?" he asked sincerely.

"I didn't belong there," I told him. "It wasn't a world meant for me. Everything was fake, plastic. People lied. All the time. I hated it."

"What about your parents?" he asked politely.

"*Especially* my parents," I answered.

The waiter arrived with two exquisitely arranged plates. Mine held sautéed trout with prosciutto and marinated Arkansas tomatoes. Martin had beef seared rare, with goat cheese and white truffle oil. A beautiful salad accompanied it.

"Darn it," I muttered, eying his salad. "Now I wish I'd gotten that." Martin lifted the small side plate and held it out to me. "I will not take your food."

"Please, I insist," Martin said, suspending the plate in the air.

"Stop, Martin, just eat your salad," I told him. "I'm fine, really." He sighed and lowered his plate, turning and raising his hand toward the waiter again. Again, with no words, he waved over his salad and toward me. The waiter spun on his heel toward the kitchen.

I stared at him and burst out laughing. "You are *impossible*, you know that?"

"Nothing is impossible," he told me, his eyes twinkling as he waved for the wine to be refilled.

* * *

It surprised me they didn't have to roll me back to the limo. After eating the mushrooms, my meal, the extra salad, and a chocolate soufflé with fresh vanilla bean ice cream, I could swear I felt my stomach pull my body off its center of gravity as the food bounced around in the wine.

"Enjoy yourself?" Martin asked as he leaned back and gazed at me, his head reclined on the leather seats. When I didn't answer, he reached out and brushed a stray hair that had fallen in front of my eyes.

"Don't do that," I said, pulling my head back and sitting up straight.

"My apologies if I stepped over a line," he said sincerely as he dropped his hand. He didn't sit up.

"Look, Martin, when I tell you I will not go out with you, it's not me being coy," I said as I turned to face him. He gazed up at me, the bemused smirk highlighting his sculpted cheekbones. "You and me? It wouldn't work."

"First, you *are* out with me," he smiled. "But okay, I'll play along. Why is that?"

"Well, you run a greyhound racetrack, for one," I pointed out. "I find what you all do there just completely offensive."

He looked surprised and was no longer smirking.

"How is what we do any different from your circus?" he asked, sitting up. "You worked at a place that made money off of animals, Fortuna. I make sure that the dogs are treated well, we find homes for them when they retire. We're a much more humane track than many."

"I bet that's not a hard list to top," I replied.

"That's not fair, is it?"

I couldn't tell him what the Magical Midway was, and so I couldn't explain to Martin why the circus I came from, with its werecreatures taking part by choice, was different. The dogs at his track didn't *have* a choice, and I knew how miserable Gideon had been. *Humane* was a low bar.

"Look, regardless, you and I wouldn't work," I told him again. "You live in a world I don't want to live in. The glamor and money and gambling and betting."

"You won't date me because of my job? Now who's being elitist?"

"It's not elitist!" I told him hotly, offended at that phrase being applied to me when I was anything but.

"It is. You aren't getting to know me for me, you're deciding whether I am worth your time based on my occupation. Whether it's a high-end occupation or a low-end occupation, you're still passing judgment on me based on what I do," Martin told me, tilting his head. "You feel you're better than me."

"I don't—"

"You do. Unless there's more than that," he said.

There was. There was the fact that I was a witch and he was a human. That I was still looking for my origin story and without that, I didn't fully know who I was. Until I knew who I was, I didn't want to get involved with anyone. For all those reasons, Martin Salvi and I were just a bad idea.

But most of all, there was something about him. Something that just seemed too good to be true.

Though I had to admit whatever it was?

He was good at hiding it. I couldn't sense anything.

"It's Gabriel Wilcox, isn't it," Martin guessed.

I frowned. "What about him?"

"He's *clearly* interested in you."

"He's never said anything about being interested in me."

"Probably because he's a coward," he told me as a faintly amused look flickered in his eyes. I turned away and looked out the window. Martin's off-the-cuff harsh condemnation of Gabriel surprised me a little. A few tense minutes went by as we passed the sign on the edge of town welcoming us back to Mystic's End.

"This isn't about anyone else other than me," I told Martin as I turned back to find him gazing at me, a quizzical look on his face. "I'm not ready. *That's* your answer. I'm not ready for a relationship, to get involved with anyone. And I'm not trying to be rude or anything, but I *don't* have to justify my choices to you."

"You're right, you don't," he nodded. "But if your answer is that you're not ready, then my response must be that you *may* be someday. And I want to make sure I'm the first thing you see when you are."

His probing eyes were dark, and pained. I sensed a flicker of real emotional turmoil in him for a moment, just a moment. Then it was gone.

"Look, I'm not telling you to stop bringing me food," I joked, trying to lighten the mood. "I mean, you don't pay for it, right? You get it free from the restaurants at the track."

Martin smiled. "Whether I pay for it, Fortuna, you're definitely worth the time and the effort. Just to clarify things and to make sure I don't overstep again—do I have your consent to continue being your friend, if I keep my hands to myself?" he asked. "I will reserve the right to continue to make my intentions clear, however. With your permission."

I knew in that limo I should say no because what he was asking wasn't really what he was asking. He had been, in effect, courting me for the past few months—and he was asking my permission to continue doing so. We both knew it.

. . .

I should have told him to just be my friend, stop flirting with me, go find someone else to sniff after. I should have said all that, locked this down and kicked it to the curb once and for all.

But Martin was right.

I didn't know when I would be ready.

And I didn't know if, when I was ready, that he wouldn't be *the one*. He was charming, and handsome, and his attention could be dazzling. I *liked* him, even though I was wary of him.

I paused, but then nodded.

The dashing operations manager held out his hand to shake.

I was relieved.

So relieved, in fact, that it didn't occur to me as I shook his hand that Martin Salvi had managed to politely, with my consent, break the rule about keeping his hands to himself just *seconds* after committing to it.

FOUR

"Look, I made it clear to Martin Salvi where he stands with me," I told Spike as he drifted around the kitchen. Gideon was loudly chewing several strips of bacon. "So you can stop making fun of me for taking advantage of him. I'm *not*."

"Yeah, yeah, yeah, whatever about the rich dude. I want to know more about Hugh Maddox. Do you really think they electrocuted him?" Spike asked, his eyes wide. I glanced from Spike, his face hungry for details, to Gideon, oblivious to all but the bacon, and rolled my eyes.

"Look, I don't know whether they electrocuted him. Or even who *they* is," I replied as I finished my plate and stepped toward the sink.

"Oh, he was electrocuted all right," my next-door neighbor Liz said as she climbed up the stairs. "Something fried him like a chicken. At least, that's what I picked up."

"What could you *possibly* have heard? It's not even 10 in the morning!" I informed her as I gestured toward the coffee machine. She nodded, and I grabbed a mug for my friend.

"Appointments at the salon start at 9 a.m., so by 10, I have all the scandal of the last twenty-four hours," Liz told me as she flopped down on a side chair near the kitchen table. "That's not even counting all the texts I got."

"This town is unbelievable," I said as I passed her a cup of coffee. "How do you people keep any secrets?"

"Oh, believe me, we keep them just fine. Anyway, speaking of *not* keeping secrets, I heard that you left the party last night with Martin Salvi. Rumor has it the two of you went out to dinner at a *swanky* restaurant in Little Rock," Liz said as she wiggled her eyebrows up and down. "Have you finally elected to give our most eligible bachelor a whirl?"

"Pepper wanted to stay and gather information on the story, so Martin just offered to drive me home, that's all."

"And he just *happened* to make a minor

deviation to a pricey restaurant in Little Rock on the way to the center of town?"

"No, he asked me if I was hungry, and I said—look, it wasn't a date or anything," I confessed while struggling not to sound defensive. "I just wasn't at the party that long before...Well, *before*. I hadn't really eaten, and so he took me to a restaurant. It's not that big of a deal."

"A fifty dollar a plate restaurant? *Known* for its romantic patio? Sure, no big deal."

I didn't reply, but I wasn't sure *why* I was so defensive with Liz about Martin Salvi. The whole town had seen him coming and going from my shop and had probably guessed he wasn't coming for painting lessons. He didn't acquire any art from the gallery, and he invariably came bearing food for two.

Martin wasn't really making *any* secret of his interest in me.

"I bet Angie will *lose her mind* when she finds out," Liz murmured into the cup. "She's been trying to get Salvi to take her to that restaurant since it opened last year."

"Martin Salvi can take anyone to any restaurant he wants. We are not involved," I told Liz pointedly. "We're just friends. He knows that I don't want to date him, *why* I don't want to go out with him, and everybody is super clear on the fact that we are not dating."

"I don't think Angie is *nearly* as clear on that point as you think."

"I don't care what she's clear on or what she's not clear on," I grumbled as I shifted away from Liz and started washing my plate in the sink. "If she's somehow jealous that Martin has a female friend, well, maybe that kind of attitude is why she's having trouble closing the deal with him."

My phone buzzed, and I wiped my hands on the dishtowel so I could pick it up. It was a text from Martin telling me he had a wonderful time last night, and that he hoped I had a good day. I put the phone down without texting him back.

"Who's that?" Liz quizzed mischievously.

"It's nobody."

"I bet it's Martin Salvi," she sing-songed.

"You *really* are impossible," I told her as I tapped the phone on the counter so the screen would blank.

"You seem to say that about many people," Liz quipped as she stood up and put her empty coffee mug in the sink. She had drained it in record time. "Me, Miss Bessie, Pepper—though, granted, Pepper *is* impossible. Miss Bessie, too, I guess...Crap, does that mean *I'm* impossible?" Liz feigned shock as she ran her hand through her purple highlighted hair.

"Stop," I scolded her.

She chuckled.

"Oh, one more thing," Liz said as she turned and leaned against the counter, crossing her arms. "It's why I came over here. There's a rumor going around that the police are looking *really* hard at the statue."

I narrowed my eyes. "What do you mean?"

"Well, the word is that the statue was rigged to electrocute anyone that touched it."

"That's absurd!"

"I'm not sure how or what they found or anything else more specific than that, but if that's *really* what they're looking at? Be ready for a visit from the police."

I jerked my head up and stared at her. "You don't mean to tell me they think *I* did this?"

"I don't really know more than what I've told you. Give me a few more appointments, I may have more dirt."

As Liz went down the steps toward the first floor, I wondered again what that silver paint was doing on my sculpture.

* * *

"Miss Delphi," the Reverend Dexter Kane drawled as he strode into my shop one hour later. "You look *remarkably* plucky for so early in the morning, young lady."

"It's almost lunchtime," I responded as I pointed to the clock. "It's not altogether what you would call *early*."

"Well, now, *I* heard that you had a late night, young woman. In Little Rock until well past midnight, was it?"

So now I was out in Little Rock past midnight, was I?

"Well, you heard wrong, Reverend. I reached home before midnight and was huddled up in my bed by the time the witching hour hit."

"In bed *after* dinner, were we?" Dexter Kane drawled, his tone full of innuendo. I could see the glimmer of yearning for details in his eyes.

The man's energy repulsed me.

"What can I do for you today, Reverend?" I asked, ignoring his rhetorical question (and the insinuation that he made with the comment). "Did you need some art supplies for the church?"

"Actually, I'm taking care of something for Della Maddox. Poor woman, left all alone in that big mansion now," he said, his face falling into an expression of well-practiced sympathy and grief. "She'd like a portrait of her husband for the funeral, one made from this picture."

Dexter Kane pulled out an 8 x 10 of a smiling

Hugh Maddox as he stood with his hands on his hips and his chest heaved out. He appeared to be on a cliff overlooking a canyon. A churning white-capped river flowed in the distant background of the ravine below him.

"When do you require this?" I asked him. "Is there any specific medium that you or Mrs. Maddox want this reproduced in?"

"Tomorrow by 6 p.m., which is when the service starts. And by medium, do you mean oils or acrylic?"

"Yes, or pastels, charcoal, watercolor. I can do it in whatever you or Mrs. Maddox wish."

"I don't think she has a preference, but let's not make it pastel colored. He was a tough man, with a *real* man's inclinations. I'd *hate* to see that portrayal of him be too...girly."

I thought about pointing out to the misogynistic man of God that just because I did a picture in the medium of pastels it didn't automatically mean it would come out in pink and baby blue, but I resolved to just let it go.

"I'll try to use stereotypically masculine colors, Reverend Kane," I deadpanned. "Do you have a size preference?"

"Well, now, dear, you look just about perfect to me. Curvy in the right places, abundant blessings where God planned them to be," the skeevy pastor said as his eyes slid toward my chest. "It's a shame," he continued as I spun away toward the blank canvas bundles, "that old Hugh didn't have a chance to admire you for excessively long, my dear. You're just his type."

What, breathing?

Ugh. I could practically feel the disgusting man's eyes on my derrière as I bent over to pull out three distinct sizes of canvas for him to choose from.

"I was speaking about the canvas for your portrait," I responded through clenched teeth as I held the three up. Their placement conveniently covered most of my frame from his lecherous stare. "What size painting would you like?"

"That big one right there," he told me as he pointed to the 24x30. "We want to make sure it's seen clearly from the back pew. Make sure that the mistresses can see it *along* with the widow," he snorted, then chuckled—slowly trailing off when I did not join in the hilarity. Dexter Kane cleared his throat. "Ah, do I pay now, or later?"

"I have a feeling a man like you prefers to pay later," I told him plainly, still holding up the canvas in front of me. The double entendre flew right past him. "I'll just send the church a bill so you won't have to stop by again."

"I'd be happy to come pick it—"

"That's all right, really," I asserted, resolved to

bring this interaction to a close, and avert another equally painful one if I could. "I'll have the painting delivered there by tomorrow at 5 p.m., along with the invoice. Anything else I can do for you, Reverend?"

We looked at one another quietly, me holding the canvas like a shield and he looking at me like a hound that *could* snag the bone he wanted if he just lunged quickly enough. After a few awkward moments, he shook his head no, and shifted toward the door.

"I appreciate the haste with which you're committing to get this done, Miss Delphi," he noted without turning around. About two feet from the door, he halted and turned his gaze toward my front stand. Kane *seemed* to gawk at the white selenite crystal ball displayed there.

"It looks like a pearl," he stammered. The fact that it did seemed to unnerve him.

"It's selenite," I called after him.

"Is it for sale?"

"No, sir," I told him. "It's mine. I've had it a long time, and wouldn't sell it at any price."

He angled toward me and raised his eyebrow. Licking his lips, he smiled—and for just a glimmer of a *flash* of a moment his expression looked so ferocious it caused my breathing to pause. The expression flickered again just as rapidly and vanished into a friendlier, but not *friendly*, expression. It happened so fast I wondered if I had seen it at all.

"*Everything* has a price, Ms. Delphi," he declared, and suddenly strode out the door just as Gideon entered the room behind me.

"Not everything," I grunted as I released the canvases. Gideon barked. "Fat good *you* are as a guard dog. You didn't perceive some kind of sinister evil coming from that dude? Really? Couldn't have come down to check on me?"

Gideon barked repeatedly, and delivered an image of himself splayed out in my unmade bed, his tongue dangling out of his mouth. A wet track of drool made a dark shape on my pillow as he snored.

*   *   *

"We only have two minutes," Pepper said as she dashed in just as I wrapped up the likeness of Hugh Maddox. No one was in the shop, so I helped the portrait along with a little magic, completing it in just twenty minutes. "Give me the silver paint, and I'll get rid of it."

"What silver paint? And *what* are you talking about?" I said as I shifted to see Pepper Stanford racing through my studio. She was picking up and setting down paint canisters one after another. "We only have two minutes until *what*, exactly?"

"The police get here with a search warrant," Pepper spat as she stumbled over a chair.

"Pepper, *slow* down, will you?" I called out as she leaped around like a meth-addicted rabbit. "Just stop rushing around like an insane woman and *tell* me what you're talking about in full sentences. Slowly. While breathing occasionally."

She swerved to a stop and turned to face me. "The police realized that the silver paint on your figure was some kind of unique, fancy, electrically conductive paint. That's how Hugh Maddox got electrocuted. The pigment was stuck on it without the sealant that goes on top to stop people from getting electrocuted when they handle it. They're blaming you. Saying it was negligence."

That *this* police department found *all* that out in fewer than twenty-four hours was *pretty* extraordinary. Frankly, the department wasn't the most notable group of crime fighters I'd ever come across.

I mean, it took them longer than Spike had been *alive* to recover his dead body in my wall.

"They're blaming me for *what*?"

"Hugh's death. The paint. Negligent homicide," she told me furiously as she started to drop verbs and nouns in the sentences she was using. Her head started to pivot on her neck as her eyes scoured the mountains of supplies.

"But *I* didn't paint the statue silver," I explained again.

"Yeah, I know you *said* that, but if the paint is *here*, they will pin it on you, anyway."

"I don't *have* any electrically conductive paint," I told her as she recovered her full speed and returned to flying around the studio. "Silver, or any other color. I didn't even know anything like that existed. So, I don't have any. Let them search if they want," I shrugged.

"That you *know* of," she frowned as she moved rolling tool chests and checked behind them. "Your store is open, anyone could wander in here and drop it here or there. You know, to frame you."

"This is ludicrous. Who would *frame* me?"

Pepper turned and stared at me, her eyes wide. "Didn't one of those idiots claim that *you* may have killed Spike *just* because you found his body? Even though you were, what, *five* at the time he disappeared?"

"Oh, come on, he wasn't serious," I scoffed, putting my hands on my waist and staring at her. Her serious expression didn't change. "How could that have been *serious*, Pepper?"

"I keep *telling* you this town is bizarre," she said as she held out her backpack stuffed with conspiracies. "Here, read it all! This isn't even the weirdest thing to happen here this *decade*, and I'm *including* the fact that you're an honest to goodness witch. Hey," she blinked, dropping the backpack. "Can't you just magic up—"

The door bells jingled, and the sound of heavy footsteps echoed.

"Damn!" she whispered. "You better hope that *you're* right and I'm wrong," Pepper said as she looked suspiciously toward the archway. "Because they're here. And if they find that paint here, *you'll* have a new address in Mystic's End on the edge of town."

Chief Clutterbuck burst into the back room barking orders at his officers. A regretful Gabe Wilcox walked up to me and held out the search warrant.

FIVE

L uckily, it wasn't boiling outside—since that's where the police ordered me to stay while they ransacked all three floors of my store and residence. Chief Clutterbuck assigned Gabe to stand watch over me and my hound.

Which, when you think about it, sounds kind of absurd. The chief had to realize that we were acquainted.

"Do you need anything? Any water? Maybe some water for Gideon?" Gabe asked sympathetically. I perched on the curb, Gideon attentively beside me, while Gabe hovered over us. "I have a bottle of water..."

"I just need this to be over with," I said to him. He nodded and glanced back toward the door.

They had been in my home for over an hour, and the officers rummaging through it were either the least excited group of individuals when finding evidence or they had turned up nothing. No calls of excitement, no *Over here!* punctuated the silent suspense.

At least they let me remain in the rear alley instead of on the front curb in the midst of the city center. I was only gawked at by the townspeople that worked at their nosiness.

"I'm sorry about this," Gabe told me softly.

"I'm not mad at you, Gabe. You're just doing your job."

"I appreciate you saying that. I thought about trying to get out of coming over here, but I realized that it *might* be better if I'm on this case," he advised me as he peered toward the window above me and nodded to someone. Looking down, Gabe smiled. "I can at least make sure you're treated objectively, if nothing else."

"*Can* you, though?" I complained to him with a raised brow. "I told you last night that I *didn't* decorate the angel silver, so if the silver paint is what you guys are looking for? You will *not* find it here. When the deliverymen picked up the statue yesterday, it was white. *Not* silver."

"I know," Gabe said as he nodded. "I disclosed what you told me last night to the chief."

"Then *what* are you doing here?" I challenged him, my arms wide. Gideon stared at Gabe and yapped.

"He still felt it was necessary to look after... Wait—how do *you* know that we're looking for the silver paint? You didn't even read the search warrant," the detective asked me, his eyes narrowing.

"I'll give you three guesses. The first two don't count."

"Pepper," Gabe suggested, and I nodded.

"She raced in here just a minute or two before you guys stomped in here like you were storming a drug house," I said as I stood up to stretch my limbs. Gabriel looked away politely as I drew my arms back, sticking my chest forward. "She mentioned the electric paint, or whatever, then."

"Conductive paint," Gabe corrected. "It carries an electric current."

"*Paint* can carry an electric current strong enough to electrocute someone?" I asked him.

"I guess," he shrugged. "I guess we'll know when we find it."

"Why not just test the paint on the statue?"

"They did, someone from Maddox Electric tested it."

"Wait—*Maddox* Electric? As in Hugh Maddox?" I asked, surprised.

"I know, weird, right? That's what you get when you live in a small town, though," Gabriel told me as he ran his hand through his hair. "Maddox owned it with a business associate, Joe Arturo. Hugh's little brother, Bob, runs it. Hugh and Joe were just the guys that made the money. They are the local electricians, so we requested some certified guys from there to test."

"That doesn't seem *odd* to you?" I asked Gabriel, my eyes narrowing. "That Hugh's work partner and brother's company is the company telling you my statue killed him?"

"Not really," Gabe shook his head. "Like I said, small town. It's not unheard of for the police department to consult with whatever experts we have in the town. If we have an art theft, we'll probably come ask you to help."

"If I'm not in jail, you mean," I pointed out.

"Well. Yeah."

Gideon whined.

* * *

"I was confident we would turn up that paint in her place," Chief Clutterbuck said to Gabe as he marched into the back alley and studied me. "But my boys have searched every inch and we have found no paint that matches the color. I guess the report we got was wrong." Despite his words, his face didn't look satisfied.

"*What* report?" I asked him.

"Never you mind what report, young woman," the chief snapped at me. "We had probable cause to search your place, otherwise we wouldn't have done it. Everything is in the search warrant," he said as he pointed to the flimsy papers I held in my hand.

I opened them up and checked the few sentences that were there. The probable cause for the search warrant was pretty light on explanation.

The papers outlined that *someone—just someone*—reported me to the police department. They—whoever they were—had seen a can of conductive paint in my studio. They didn't leave their name. It didn't even specify whether the person reporting this incredibly specific nugget of information was a male or female, called or stopped by. Did they send a telegram? Smoke signals, maybe?

Nothing.

Someone said something about something they saw, and the MEPD got a warrant to search my place. If this has been a *Law & Order* episode, Sam Waterston's character would yell at someone about corruption or something.

I suppose we had Pepper for that here.

"You don't think this is pretty thin?" I asked him, shaking the papers.

"A judge thought it was just fine," Chief Clutterbuck said as he crossed his arms. "We took nothing, we broke nothing, and you're not getting arrested, so I don't see what you have to fret about," he advised me haughtily.

"You don't see—" I started indignantly, but Gabe grabbed my arm and stepped in front of me.

"Is Fortuna allowed back inside now, chief?"

"What?" he asked Gabe, even though he continued to glare at me sharply. Gabe repeated the question. "Oh, yes, yes, that's fine," he said with a swing of his hand. "I'm sure she wants to get back in there and clean up the revolting mess her dog made. Filthy beast," the chief muttered as he glowered from me to Gideon.

Gideon didn't look disturbed by the chief of police's attitude in the slightest. In fact, he wagged his tail.

"Are you coming back to the station with us, Wilcox? Or are you planning on staying here with the suspect?"

"If you found nothing, how am I a suspect?" I quizzed him.

"Just because we found nothing doesn't mean there wasn't anything to find," the chief responded, seemingly blind to the implicit admittance of his own staff's incompetence contained within his statement. "Someone will discover it eventually, and when they do, I have a cell with Ms. Delphi's name on it."

"Do you, now?" Martin Salvi asked as he strode up to the four of us. "Chief Clutterbuck," he nodded and held out his hand to shake. "Detective Wilcox," Martin nodded without extending his hand. "What's going on here, chief?"

"Your girlfriend is a suspect in a murder—"

"Surely not," Martin answered with a smile.

"I'm not his girlfriend," I declared to the chief.

"Surely not," Gabe muttered, and I nudged him.

"What are you doing here?" I asked Martin.

"Word travels fast, and I was worried about you. Perhaps next time I should send you a text wishing you a lousy day instead—if you're determined to have the opposite," Martin grinned as he stepped around and in front of Gabe. "Have you requested a lawyer?"

"What do I need a lawyer for?" I asked him, startled.

"Well, I doubt any lawyer worth his salt would have tolerated a search like this based on such flimsy evidence," Martin replied as he reached for the search warrant and flipped through the two pages. "An anonymous phone call? Surely you have better than this, Clutterbuck. And you," Martin said as he gestured toward Gabe and glared. "I thought *you* were her friend."

"I have a job to do—"

"And we *all* know what kind of job the MEPD is known for, don't we?" Martin's nose twitched as he shot a bitter glance at Gabe. In response, Gabe's face turned bright crimson.

"You *would* know, wouldn't you, Salvi?" Gabe responded with an insulted expression.

"Now, lads, she's hardly worth all this, is she?" Chief Clutterbuck said to the two men with scarcely concealed amusement as I observed the three of them posture, preen, and struggle to overshadow one another. I fought the urge to bite the chief's head off.

Martin and Gabe continued to lock eyes, fierce energy crackling between the two of them. The chief cleared his throat and studied his detective. "Gabe, we heard the word lawyer, so maybe it's a better idea that you come back to the station with me and leave her in the hands of Mr. Salvi."

"I have two hands of my own, thank you very much," I told Chief Clutterbuck as I stepped away from the testosterone circle. "I don't need to be left with anyone. I can take care of myself."

"You've only been here three months, Ms. Delphi, and this is the second time we're at your home. Rethink that assumption," the chief advised me arrogantly as he turned on his heel and went back into my shop.

"Jerk," I sputtered. Gideon barked, and I looked down at him. "Again, I'd like to point out you're kind of a crappy guard dog. No growl? No bark? Not even a serious glance at that guy while baring your teeth?"

Gideon stood up, wagged his tail, and leaned against me.

"I have to go, but before I do," Gabe said as he turned his back on Martin and put his hands on my shoulders. "Don't trust him."

"Your boss? I wouldn't trust him as far as I could comfortably spit a rat," I assured him as I shrugged off his hands. "No problem."

"Not him," Gabe said, and he jerked his head over his shoulder toward Martin. "Him. Don't trust him."

"I didn't just search her lingerie drawer based on a BS warrant, Wilcox," Martin countered, untroubled by Gabe's proclamation. "I expect you're projecting a bit. Or you're envious."

"Fortuna, please...Don't trust him," Gabe said again, ignoring Martin's polite taunts. "I'll call you later and check on you."

"You can call her lawyer," Martin said as he stepped forward and put his arm around me. The two thick-bodied men, muscles tense, glared at each other fiercely. "But while *you're* investigating this potential homicide and *she's* a suspect? *You* don't talk to her. If you do? I guarantee you, I'll have your badge."

Gabe Wilcox turned on his heel and walked away furiously, going back into my shop after his boss. The door closed with a slam.

* * *

As soon as the police left, Martin led me back into my shop. Within moments, Liz and Pepper ran in the front to see if I was okay. I thought.

"I just kind of melted into the background when they came in as if I was a customer," Pepper told me as she dashed to my side. I thought for a second she would give me a hug, but as soon as she was within reach, she yanked the search warrant out of my hand and began examining it.

"I'm *fine*, by the way," I called to her as she walked away, her eyes buried in the few words on the page. "In case you're wondering, I'm not hurt. Gideon's okay. I wasn't detained. They claim they didn't break anything. In case you were interested."

No response from Pepper.

"I would've asked all those questions," Liz

smiled as she wandered over and offered me a hug. "I am overjoyed you're all right. What on earth were they searching for?"

"Paint. Silver paint," I told her as I scanned around the workshop. The police may not have broken anything, but they clearly had no idea how things were set up. Acrylic brushes were mixed in with watercolor brushes, oil and acrylic paints were thrown in buckets. I sighed. "It will take me days to reorganize this."

"No, it won't, I'm confident you can just wiggle your fingers," Pepper murmured as she squinted at the signature on the page.

"What do you mean, wiggle her fingers?" Liz asked, baffled by her statement. Martin looked at Pepper, his face stoic.

"What?" she inquired as she glanced up. "What was your question?"

"Oh, never mind, not important," Liz said as she stepped toward the stairs. "Let's check your apartment."

"Before you do that, I'd like you to let me hire you a lawyer," Martin said as he caught my arm tightly. "I keep the best firm in the county on retainer, and if you'll permit me, I'd like to call them for you and assign one of them to this."

"I can pay for my own attorney, but I don't think I need one," I told him impatiently as I shook my arm from his grasp. "I appreciate what you're trying to do, Martin, but—"

"This shouldn't have happened," he announced, his tone crisp and his gaze...It looked almost dangerous. "This was an abuse, and I won't permit it to happen to you again."

"*I'm sorry—you* won't *permit?*" I demanded incredulously, and to my shock he burned at my words. "You won't *permit?* I assume you're taking some of those liberties we chatted about. You know, the ones you *don't* have?"

"Oh, boy, you're in trouble now," Pepper breathed without glancing up.

"Pepper, let's go upstairs," Liz turned back and grabbed Pepper's arm.

"But, wait, I want to see—"

"Upstairs," Liz told her as she pulled her toward the landing. "You want to see upstairs. And you want to see it right now."

"Fine," Pepper reluctantly agreed. Turning to me, she pointed her finger. "But you better remember what you say to him so you can tell me later, or you need to yell at him loud enough that I can hear on the second floor. Deal?"

"Pepper!" Liz said sharply, pointing at the second floor with one hand while she tugged on Pepper with the other.

"Oh, all right!"

I turned back to Martin. The flush of... embarrassment? It had faded from his face, and his expression was back to the typical serious bemusement. "I don't like that," I told him emphatically.

"What, precisely?" Martin inquired, his head bending. "My attempt to take care of you? My inclination to watch out for you? My desire to look after you?"

"You know, you're trying to make it sound all sweet and nice and positive, but it's possessive, Martin," I told him, and his eyes grew ever so slightly. "It's possessive, as if you're choosing *for* me, and I don't like it. I want you to stop."

"I'm sorry, I was just trying to—"

"You don't own me," I told him. "I'm *not* yours."

"Not yet," he gave a half smile and stepped closer to me.

I stepped backward. "See? *That*. That right there, that assumption, it's just so—"

"Confident?" he smiled fully.

"Arrogant," I told him, frowning.

"I can't help what I feel, Fortuna."

"You *can* help what you do. You're a grown man. I've asked you to stop, and you've agreed to stop. We've drawn the lines of where I'm comfortable with you going, and where I'm not," I told him as I crossed my arms. "If you can't respect that, then maybe we can't be friends."

His face fell. "Now, wait a minute—"

"This is the second time I've had to say something in as many days," I cut him off. "You've had *two* warnings. The third won't be a warning."

Martin stared at me, incredulous. "You can't be serious."

"You *don't* want to try me on that," I responded. "I really like you, Martin. Someday, maybe, I might even be ready to go out with you. But that's *not* today, and until it is? You'll respect me and my boundaries or you'll go. It's your choice."

He continued staring at me for a few seconds longer and then turned slowly and walked out the front door.

I sighed, missing the shrimp scampi already.

SIX

Liz and Pepper were standing in the center of the living room checking the floorboards. At the sound of my footsteps, Pepper's gaze rose.

"I didn't even hear you yell, so where is he?" Pepper asked as I strode onto the landing and into the kitchen.

"Martin? He took off."

"Why?" Liz asked, her eyes darting to the stairs as if she didn't quite believe it.

"I reminded him of boundaries he agreed to respect that he wasn't, in fact, adhering to," I told her, holding up my hand toward Pepper to head off any further queries. "I don't want to talk about my absent love life—did you guys find anything here?"

"Not really," Liz told me, shaking her head. "I mean, clearly they scoured through stuff up here, but it doesn't really look like there was a focal point. They were just turning over every rock."

"We haven't gone up to your bedroom yet," Pepper said as she nodded toward the second stairway. "We both decided having ten men plodding through your bedroom was enough violation for one day. I mean," Pepper shrugged, "unless you're *into* that sort of thing."

"I'm not," I stared at her.

"Yeah, well, I don't know, you're hanging with the town bad-ass and all," Pepper pointed out. "You may *like* 'em dark and dangerous. Who am I to pass judgment?"

"This town only has one bad-ass, and Martin's it? I may have only been here three months now, but I find *that* really hard to believe."

The second floor smelled faintly of uber-masculine cologne and body spray, no doubt from the police department's search team. I crossed the room and opened the window closest to the square to let some fresh air in and some malodorous man-cloud out. Looking down, I could see townspeople assembled, whispering, in front of the old courthouse.

"Great," I exhaled. "I'm the town curiosity once again."

"Oh, we all take a turn, Fortuna," Liz said as she patted me on the back and looked out into the street. Then she frowned. "Hey, I wonder what Angie's doing here. She doesn't have an appointment today."

Sure enough, as I scanned the townspeople, I spotted Evangeline Laroux leaning against the hood of her limousine as if she were awaiting her close-up in a rock video. Her sunglasses hid her eyes as she gazed up at my home. The awkward looking young man I had seen at the Maddoxes' party stood beside her looking glum.

"Maybe *she* was the one that called and turned me in," I said as she shook hands with a townsperson, and then posed for a selfie. "It wouldn't shock me. That woman seems to loathe me."

"How do you know it was a phone call?" Pepper asked as she checked the search warrant and then peered back up at me. "Did Chief Clutterbuck tell you the report was a phone call?"

I thought a minute. "No—"

"Gabe?"

I shook my head and tried to recall where I got the idea the anonymous report was a phone call. Then it hit me. "No, actually, Martin mentioned it when he walked up to us in the back alley."

"Martin Salvi?" I nodded at Pepper. "Did he say that just to *you*, or to everyone?"

"To everyone. Me, Gabe, Clutterbuck—"

"Did Gabe or Clutterbuck argue with him or correct him at all?" Pepper asked, staring at me keenly. I felt uneasy at her questions.

"I think you're reading way too much into this. Maybe he just misspoke," I told her, shifting from one foot to another. "Or just expected it was a phone call because of the way they wrote the search warrant."

"Sure. Or maybe he knew something," Pepper said, crossing her arms. "You're *really* trusting for someone that's able to read people's minds, you know."

I glowered at her as I thought back to the exchange, and as much as I wanted to knock Pepper for being paranoid again, the scene began nagging at me. As I played it over once, twice, in my mind, I realized that Martin said something about the phone call before he'd even laid eyes on the papers.

I revealed what I remembered to her, my shoulders drooping just a bit. Yes, Martin was a bit over the top in some ways, but I didn't really believe he—or anyone in this town, really—was as malevolently crooked as Pepper always believed.

But...it was a little odd.

"I distinctly remember that he was reaching for

the papers. But, come on, Pepper—the way this town gossips? Maybe he just heard it somewhere," I told her, trying to convince myself nothing peculiar was going on.

You know, aside from the dead guy and me getting blamed for it.

"Okay, sure, that's *possible*," she said as she began pacing. Liz followed the two of us, her eyes wide. "But why would he take you to Little Rock for dinner just *last* night, of all nights?"

"Hold on, are you now insisting *that* was planned?" I challenged her. "You think he's weaseled into my life the past three months just so he could take me out after a murder so...what, someone *else* could cast suspicion on me? Or are you suggesting he did it all?"

"Look, she *wasn't* really framed," Liz pointed out. "Someone just made a phone call and said she had some paint. She didn't. They didn't find any paint."

Gideon barked and wagged his tail. His limbs flexed, and he scampered toward the stairs going up to my bedroom. Looking back at me, he wagged his tail harder. "Not now, Gideon," I told him, turning back toward Liz. "I get what you're—"

Gideon let loose a string of barks, so boisterous that I couldn't even talk over them.

"*What*, Gideon?" He barked again, hopped up

on the stairs, bolted down, and wagged his tail. He jammed a vision of all of us walking up the steps, hard, into my mind.

"Ow," I told him. "That hurt, dog."

He barked.

"He wants us to go upstairs," I explained to them.

"Um, yeah, we can see *that*," Pepper told me sharply.

Liz was gawking at me as if something about this exchange had tickled a question in the back of her mind that she was unwilling to ask. Pulling her eyes away, she strolled toward Gideon.

"Let's see what he wants to show us," she recommended, her manner relaxing a bit as she followed him up.

* * *

"Gideon!" I hollered as I encountered the smelly pile of dog poo on top of my freshly washed laundry. I leaned down at the knocked over hamper and stared. "Did you knock it over, or did the police?" I asked him. "Bad dog!"

He thrust an image in my head of him standing tall, a medal of honor pinned to his collar.

"No, Gideon, this was *not* good. You are *not* a good dog," I told him as I reached out carefully to move the clothing toward the trash bin. As I lifted the soiled pile, a can glinted. "Wait a minute..."

Silver paint had dripped and dried along the rim of the can. I froze, astonished. Gideon barked as he sat next to me looking as cocky as he could be. "Did you do this?" I asked the dog. He leaned forward and licked my face, wagging his tail more.

"That's one *smart* dog," Pepper murmured as she leaned down and peered at the paint can. Turning to me, she raised an eyebrow. "I will presume you've never seen it before, but I have to ask. Do you know what this is?"

"No. I mean, it looks like a can of house paint," I told her. "It doesn't look like anything I've ever ordered before."

"And it doesn't have a label, so we can't even track it," Pepper said with a grimace. Standing up, she turned to me and looked down as she wrote something in her ever-present notepad. "This doesn't really bode well for your relationship with Money-bucks Martin. I just wanted to touch on that," she informed me.

"Did the police really not find what they were searching for just because they were too squicked out to move dog poop?" Liz asked, her voice skeptical. "I mean, it's just dog poop—wait, are you throwing those clothes away?" she demanded as she observed me drop two tunics and a pair of trousers into the garbage.

"What? *You* want to clean it?" I challenged her as I pointed toward the trash.

"Oh, crap—no pun intended—I have an appointment," Liz said as she sighted the clock on the wall. "I'll be back in a flash."

"Don't you tell anyone what we found!" Pepper called after her severely.

"What am I, a moron?" she asked as she hopped down the stairs. "Catch me up when I get back!"

* * *

"Okay, now that we're alone, where's Spike?" Pepper asked hastily.

"Liz knows I can see ghosts, remember? As for Spike, I don't know, I—"

"Can't he *not* leave here?" she fired back, interrupting me.

"I thought so, but—

"What else did the dog tell you?"

"Nothing, he just—"

"How did someone get in here without the ghost *or* the dog noticing, all the way up to your bedroom?" Pepper asked skeptically as her head whirled around.

"Well, I don't know, let me—"

"And did Martin Salvi say anything—"

"Pepper!" I yelled, so emphatically that Gideon jumped. "*Slow down*, will you? You're not letting me deal with any questions," I told her as I wandered over to the bed and sat down. "Just let me think a minute, will you?"

"Well, hurry," she declared as she twirled her pencil quickly in my direction. "Liz will be back here in an hour, so if we're going to use any of your magic stuff, we have a minimal amount of time to do it."

My eyes narrowed. "What do you mean, use my magic stuff?"

"Oh, come on, you must have something in that magic arsenal of yours that will reveal who left that paint can in your house," Pepper said. "Some spell that will show you what transpired last night? Some magic wand that will raise fingerprints? Something?"

"I told you, magic isn't the answer to everything," I said as my eyes darted around the bedroom to see if anything else was missing. With relief, I saw the small communication cauldron still resting on my bedside table. It was the easiest way for me to get help from the other witches I knew, now that I was living in a place where I was the only one, and I was glad they didn't take it or break it.

"Yeah, I hear you, but it is the answer *sometimes*, you know. Otherwise, why would it survive?"

"I keep telling you, I'm the least of witches," my nose scrunched. "I don't know as much as you give me credit for. I spent most of my life being a telepath, and even now, Pepper, the main thing I work on is keeping out of people's heads."

"Yeah, yeah, I know, privacy and sovereignty and permission and blah blah blah," she scowled as she rolled her eyes. "Just my luck I become friends with the only witch trying to roll *back* her powers instead of expand them."

"I'm not trying to roll *back* my powers, just trying to use them more ethically," I murmured, thinking. "Gideon," I said, turning to look at the dog. "I haven't seen Spike, but *you* were here all night last night while I was out. Did *you* see someone bring that can up here?"

Gideon barked.

"Why didn't you tell me when I got home that someone had broken into the place and hid paint?" I asked him, perplexed.

The image of a festively-wrapped present with a gigantic bow appeared in my mind.

"You thought someone was giving me a gift?"

Gideon barked.

"I think he figured out that it wasn't a gift when

the police got here," I told Pepper. "That must be when he dragged the clothing over the can and...ah, ensured the police really wouldn't want to touch it."

"Can he show you what he saw, and then you do that paint image thing with your wiggly fingers?" Pepper asked, referring to one of the few acts of magic I was great at—reproducing something I saw onto a canvas with magic.

I had asked Pepper once not to talk about magic in front of people. To call it something else, just so we weren't overheard. She picked wiggly or fidget fingers. I didn't *need* to wiggle my fingers to cast a spell, but...well, I did. It was a habit I picked up from Gunther.

"I can try. Gideon?" My mind filled with a yellow-gray image, hazy. "Gideon, I can barely see the guy," I told him as I saw a black blob creep through my bedroom.

Gideon barked and crammed a rapid-fire series of pictures at me. After processing all the information Gideon was trying to impart, I turned to Pepper. "I'm not sure this will help us. If something is fresh in my mind, Gideon can send it to me the way I would see it—because he sees it in my head and figures out how to mirror it to get his point across."

"Okay," Pepper said.

"Him sending me a figure *he* saw that I haven't? It's dog vision."

"Okay, so?"

"Dogs don't see all that clearly," I told her. "It's vague, like an out-of-focus image."

"Isn't he a *sight* hound?" Pepper asked incredulously.

"He is, but that doesn't mean he has human perception, just better vision than other dogs," I explained to her. "Greyhounds have an elongated visual streak," I pointed out, grateful that Irma Sperling, the town librarian, had stocked the shelves with greyhound books so I could sound like I knew what I was talking about. "It gives them a panoramic view of the ground when they run and—"

"Okay, thanks for the greyhound lesson," Pepper said as she scratched Gideon's head. "Back to the form of whoever came up here. Do it anyhow. *Maybe* we'll be able to spot something that'll help us figure out who it is. Even if it's out of focus."

"Let's go to the studio," I answered as Pepper stopped scratching Gideon and advanced toward the stairs.

SEVEN

"It's a blob," I said as we stared at the canvas. "It's a sinister, shadowy blob."

"Don't get your panties in a bunch, Delphi. It's not just a *blob*," Pepper said as she surveyed the painting closely. "It's presumably a man. That's your dresser and judging by where the head is, he's probably about 5'10". So, not a tall man."

"You can tell *all* that from that blob?" I asked her, pointing to the black, gray, and green haze I had just painted magically.

"Look," she replied as she put down her notebook and turned her back on the canvas. "I *know* what you think of me. Hell, I know what *everybody* in this town thinks of me," Pepper said as she scratched absently at her head. "Crazy Pepper, tin-foil hat lady. I know that everyone assumes I'm a joke—"

"Pepper, I categorically *don't* think you're a joke. Not at all," I told her. "You're passionate. And you don't think thoroughly before you speak or act. You plow over people like they're snow from a blizzard and you're resolved to gather it all in one pass."

My friend's look of injured innocence was diminishing as I talked, and a half smile broke her bleak expression.

"But I don't interrupt you to make you stop, and I don't challenge you because I don't believe you. You have trouble concentrating, and occasionally poking you to defend your assertions is the quickest way to make you focus and clarify what you mean," I confessed to her. "That's all."

"That's *all*?" she asked suspiciously.

"Okay, granted, sometimes you drive me a little crazy and I just want to shut you up," I conceded. "But that doesn't mean I think you're a joke."

"Yeah, I get that," she nodded. "The drive people crazy part. It's not like I don't know I'm a bit much to take," Pepper agreed.

"Besides, I'm the crazy lady that paid fifty thousand dollars for a pet greyhound and had a body in her wall," I told her. "It's not like you've cornered the market on weird Mystic's End stuff, you know."

"*Speaking* of that," she said as she turned around and snatched her Moleskine. "Did Spike see anything?"

"I don't know," I told her as I scanned around the room. "I haven't seen him since I got back from dinner with Martin. It's bizarre, actually. I even checked the roof. I think he must have left the building."

"Great, the one time we needed him to be Super-Glued here, he's off gallivanting around town."

"He could have moved on, you know," I pointed out, shifting back to look at the portrait. "But I sense he's still around, someplace. I think I'd feel it if he wasn't here anymore. Hey—what's that?" I pointed to a faint spot on the man-blob.

Pepper squinted. "A patch, maybe? Oh, and one more question," she turned to squint at me. "Did you see Hugh's ghost? Like, can we talk to him and ask him questions like you did with Spike?"

"I didn't," I told her. "Not everybody who passes on can be seen. It hinges a lot on what people expected death would be when they were alive, how they died—"

"Explain?" she said, sitting back down, her pen poised.

"Well, if you think that you just poof into non-existence, maybe that's what you'll experience. At least for a while. If you believe that you go to heaven, you will. If you understand you may go to hell, you might. If you believe you'll go to the Elysian fields, you will—"

"Wait, are you saying every single myth, *every* single afterlife belief, is credible?" Pepper asked, astounded.

"Not...not really. But sort of," I said, struggling to explain. "Death is a part of life. We have nine months to come into this world, right? Well, we have nine months to adjust to leaving it. Some people may not need that, but it's there if they do."

"But Spike's been here for over twenty years."

"Some people take longer," I shrugged. "There are no hard and fast rules."

"There have to be *some*—"

"Why?" I asked her, curious.

"Because there has to be *truth*," she observed.

"What *is* truth?" I asked her, my eyes twinkling.

"You're messing with me," she blinked, her face a study in skepticism. Which, to be fair, wasn't all that distinct from her normal face.

"Okay, you're right, I'm messing with you," I told her, deliberately moving away from the metaphysical discourse we had started.

Truthfully, I didn't have conclusive answers to

the questions she was asking. Even for those of us with magic and psychic powers, the world was a mystical place.

"Thanks," Pepper's eyes glistened. "You got me. Most people don't."

"The long and the short of it is I don't know where Spike is. Hopefully, he'll turn up soon."

* * *

It had been a long day. I heated up a can of soup for dinner, too spent to think about cooking anything more elaborate. (Okay, I cooked nothing more elaborate even when I felt better, but let's just blame this on a long day, anyway.) Between the exchange with Reverend Sleazy Kane and the confrontation with Martin *and* the search warrant served on me by Gabe, my energy was depleted.

"What do you think, Gideon?" I asked the dog as he patiently waited for his dinner by my side. "Is Pepper right? Could Martin be a bad guy?"

An image of Martin petting his head and giving him bacon.

"You know just because someone gives you bacon doesn't make them a good person, right?"

An image of an award ribbon with *Good Person* written on it—next to a mammoth plate of bacon.

"I wish telling good people from bad people

were as easy as that, Gideon," I responded as I opened the microwave and pulled out my bowl of soup. Staring at it, I sighed.

I missed shrimp scampi.

Gideon pressed his head and neck against my leg and gave a little deep-throated moan. I looked down and grinned at him, nudging him back. Then he barked.

"You're a very sweet dog, you know that?" Gideon wagged his tail. "But you're still not getting a giant plate of bacon for dinner," I continued as I pulled out Gideon's bowl and put in the high quality dog food. "It's not healthy to eat that much all the time."

Gideon's tail drooped, and he whimpered.

As he and I settled in for dinner, the absence left by the missing punk ghost was obvious. The house was silent, too silent. I used to prefer the quiet—it was my search for silence that lead me to take up painting at the Magical Midway.

Now, it seemed stifling. Ominous.

I started when the buzzer on the door clanged.

"I wonder who that could be?" I asked Gideon as he gobbled down the rest of his dinner in two bites and rushed down the stairs, yapping. "I wasn't expecting anyone."

As I walked across the studio and out into the storefront, I spotted Miss Bessie (Gabriel Wilcox's boisterous grandmother) glaring intently at me, Claire (her caretaker) at her side.

Gideon skidded to a stop, twisted, and flew back upstairs.

"Thanks, dog!" I called after him. "Wimp."

"Why are you and Gabe not communicating?" Miss Bessie snapped at me before I had fully opened the door. "He advised me that some man told him not to come around anymore. What is this, elementary school?"

"Good evening, Miss Bessie. Claire," I nodded as Claire helped Miss Bessie to the seating area at the front of the store and then turned around to leave. "Wait, where are you going?"

"I'll be outside in the car," Claire said in her mild way despite her rough, butch-looking exterior. "Miss Bessie wants to speak to you alone, and she suggested I wait in the car."

Sure, I could *imagine* what a *suggestion* from Miss Bessie would look like.

"And you *agreed*?" I asked, somewhat panicked.

"I'll be right outside if she needs me," Claire said as she pulled the door open. Turning back, she added softly, "Or if you need me."

"Get out, woman! Go!" Bessie barked. Claire left.

"Now, listen here, mystic," Bessie said ominously as she leaned forward, pointing her skinny finger in my direction. "You sit down in that chair right there. You and I are going to have a talk."

"I was just in the middle of my dinner," I said as I took a step toward the back. "Do you mind if I grab my—"

"You grab that chair and put your keister in it!" Bessie cried. "The wheel of the year has turned far enough without you coming to talk to me! That ends tonight!"

I paused, mulling over my options.

I could go get my soup, but that would just incense Miss Bessie and give her more time to build up a better head of steam. I also wasn't altogether convinced that the old woman wouldn't try to follow me, so full of ruthless determination was her face. I didn't want her to get hurt.

Or I could sit.

I sat.

She grinned triumphantly for a flash and suddenly grimaced.

"I whacked you and made you the town's official mystic three months ago," Miss Bessie snapped at me, her hand slapping her thigh. "You haven't come to see me once. Not once!"

"I've been to the nursing home to teach art—"

"Do you *really* think we're going to talk about this in front of those gossiping ninnies?" she yelled, rolling her eyes and clutching her chest. "Oy, girl, have *you* got a lot to learn!"

The fact was, I *had* been avoiding Miss Bessie.

Initially, I moved to Mystic's End because it was the town they had discovered me abandoned in. Just days old, on the steps of the old courthouse in the center of town. I had moved here to find the truth of my birth. To find out who I was. Why I had psychic powers in a world full of powerless humans.

At least, that's what I understood. I thought I was ready.

When Miss Bessie could see ghosts like I could, when she declared that she recognized who I was, why I came, and what I was searching for...It sounded like all I had sought was right there for the taking. Right in front of me. All I had to do was go call on her.

Which...I did not.

Even after she whacked me, turning over some power and declaring me the mystic of Mystic's End (which sounded more like a curse than a promotion), I didn't go ask her what that power was.

In fact, I ignored it.

I ignored her.

Well, I didn't *ignore* her. I was impeccably courteous to her when I saw her in public. I just didn't seek her out privately.

It turned out she had come to the end of her tolerance for *that*.

"Why did you never come to see me?" she asked slightly less sharply as she leaned back and narrowed her eyes.

"I don't know," I told her softly.

"Bull," she fired back harshly. I blinked. "You know why you've been dodging me all this time. If you're going to do it, at least be straightforward about it. If not with me, then with *yourself*."

I shifted restlessly in my chair, the weight of the old woman's gaze pressing on me. I felt oddly light-headed. She examined me closely with watery eyes as if she could see the paralysis gripping my soul.

"I'm not ready," I announced.

Her face softened, and she nodded.

"I felt when I came here that I wished for the answers. But I'm still establishing a life here. I'm not sure I'm ready to confront...whatever it is you know about me. I'm just not ready."

"Honest, at least," she informed me, and then exhaled. "Is there anything you want to know right now?"

"Am I related to you? I don't need to know how," I added quickly. "I'd just like to know whether we are."

"In what way?" she asked. I blinked again.

"By blood," I explained to her. "I mean, what other way is there?"

"Do you want that question answered, too?"

I thought about it for a moment and then nodded.

"No, we are not related by blood," Miss Bessie said. "And you are not related to Gabe," she continued as she leaned forward. "So you can stop worrying if I'm trying to force you into some *Game of Thrones* incest thing."

I flinched.

"As for how people can be related in other respects, energy connects witches. The closer the energy, the closer the coven. The tighter the link," Miss Bessie said, a distant look in her eye. "Those bonds can be more intimate than blood."

She smiled sympathetically at me as the remote look passed. "You are not blood related to any of the men in this town, Fortuna. That, at least, I can tell you."

I felt an extraordinary measure of relief at her word—even if it just made the Martin-Gabe situation more convoluted.

"Though if you preferred to be related to me," Miss Bessie said, the sympathy in her voice snapping back to the caustic tone she ordinarily used, "there's an incredibly easy way to take care of that, young lady. Just marry my Gabriel!"

"Miss Bessie, we're not even dating—"

"Well, who's fault is *that*?" she said as she peered at me rather critically. "I'm not going to be around *forever*, you know, and I'd like to look in the eyes of at least one grand-baby!"

"I'm not dating anyone right now," I told her. "Though I'll admit, your information has made it a bit easier for me if and when I decide to do so."

"Oh, please, the whole town *knows* that you've been dating that Martin Salvi fella," Miss Bessie said as she waved her hand at me dismissively. "How you could pick him over my Gabriel is beyond me!"

"I haven't picked anyone over anyone!" I told her hotly.

Her expression shifted back into the kind old woman I had just spoken to, giving me emotional whiplash. "In any case, Fortuna, when you're ready to hear your story, I'm here." Bessie smiled widely. "I won't force it on you unless you ask. Maybe now you can stop avoiding me."

"I'm not—"

"You are, but it's all right," she told me. With a frown, she continued. "I know that you didn't feel you fit in with your adoptive family, and I am truly sorry about that. I hope that you'll find your place with us here, as strange a place as it may be. It's always been here for you. Waiting."

"Thanks, Miss Bessie," I answered, and she smiled.

"Now, when are you going to go out with my Gabriel!" she snapped, slapping her hand on her thigh again. "Grand-babies, Fortuna! Grand-babies!"

EIGHT

When Gabriel Wilcox walked into my shop the following morning, I couldn't help but hear the ring of Miss Bessie's demand for grandchildren in his steps. If Gabe knew about the visit the night before, he didn't let on.

I sure didn't tell him.

"No classes?" he inquired as he glanced around at the silent shop.

"It's surprising how being suspected of killing someone with a sculpture can stop an art business cold, Detective," I told him as I laid down my magazine and leaned back on the stool behind the counter. "Haven't had a customer since Dexter Kane yesterday morning."

"Dexter Kane?" Gabe asked, startled.

"Della wanted a likeness made of Hugh for the funeral, so he hired me to do it."

Gabe nodded.

"So, is this visit business or pleasure?" I asked him.

"It's personal, sort of," Gabriel said as he shifted and peeked out the window to see if anyone was heading toward the store. "Pepper made a FOIA request for the—"

"FOIA?"

"Freedom of information request. She asked for a copy of the call that reported the paint was here, and I pulled it for the request," Gabe said as he turned uneasily, checking behind him one more time. "It was Evangeline Laroux. Well, I mean, the caller didn't say it was Ms. Laroux. But her voice... it's fairly singular. I would know it anywhere."

"Can't you all trace the call? To make sure it's her?"

"It came from the complex," he told me, shrugging. "There are so many phones there it'd be impossible to put one person at some of those numbers without security footage."

"Which you have no reason to ask for."

"Oh, we can *ask*," Gabriel said. "Martin wouldn't give it to us. In any case, I don't think it's necessary. I know it was her."

We stared at one another. It didn't shock me that Evangeline was the one that called to put me square in the middle of the latest farce. It surprised me that Gabriel Wilcox came over here by himself to tell me about it, though.

"Okay," I told him. "Out of curiosity, when did she make the call?"

"Night before last at 10:30 p.m., just two hours after Hugh passed on," Gabriel said.

I frowned.

"What?" he asked, leaning forward.

"Did you guys even know about this electrified paint thing at that point? Had the police figured that out yet?"

Now Gabriel frowned. "No, actually. We didn't realize the paint was conductive until the next morning when Ollie examined it."

"And no one was suspicious that Evangeline Laroux seemed to know about it before you?" I asked him as I stepped over to the ornate coffee maker in the shop and poured myself a large cup of coffee. "Like, no one in your *entire* police station asked yourselves why you were following a tip called in against someone when the tip itself showed some kind of insider knowledge?"

"First, the entire police station *didn't* know the specifics or the timing of the call—"

"*You* did before you got here," I reasoned out as

I handed him a coffee. "It didn't occur to you."

"Well, no, but I *know* Angie."

"You just said you *didn't* know it was Angie until you pulled the call today," I said. "So the fact that *you* know her couldn't be a factor. Unless someone else *did* know and just didn't put it on the search warrant for their own reasons."

"It could be that the boss just didn't want his own daughter involved. Maybe he talked to her about it and he knows," Gabe said, referencing Chief Clutterbuck's familial relationship with the platinum blonde.

"Maybe," I told him.

I recognized that Evangeline Laroux smoldered slinky sexuality like most women breathe, but it impressed me at how efficient that was at short-circuiting men's brains.

T he shop phone rang, and I held up my hand toward him as I reached for the receiver. "Mystic Moon Gallery, how can I help you?"

"Fortuna, it's Martin. Please don't hang up on me."

"I have no intention of hanging up on you, Martin. You were the one that stalked out of here yesterday," I told him. Gabriel raised his eyebrow. "What can I do for you?"

"Is Gabriel Wilcox questioning you?" Martin asked, his tone tight.

"Do you have someone watching me?" I challenged him, turning toward the front of the shop. My eyes scoured the sidewalk and street, but no one stood out as obviously watching me and reporting back to Martin. That he could have someone observing me and reporting back to him made me uncomfortable.

"I do not," Martin said, exhaling. Gabriel looked at me, his brows knitted together with worry. "Old Joe just showed up here for lunch and he mentioned that when he rode through town, he saw Detective Wilcox going into your shop. Alone."

"I swear, this town," I whispered as I gestured for Gabriel to follow me into the back studio. "I'm going to have the windows tinted and put in privacy screens. Yes, he's here, and it's fine—"

"Have you gotten an attorney?"

"I don't need one. I did nothing illegal."

I heard Martin mutter a string of curses. "I'll be right over," he said, and he hung up on me.

I stared at the phone and looked at Gabe.

"Salvi?"

"On his way," I told Gabe.

"That man—"

"Stop," I told him, holding my hand up. "Let him get here. I've had about enough of whatever this is between the two of you. Wait until he gets here. Then we'll all talk."

I recognized I thought differently about the two men today after speaking to Miss Bessie last night. Romance had been totally off the table for me yesterday afternoon due to the simple fact that I could be connected (without knowing how) to any of the men wandering around in Mystic's End.

Now, I was connected to neither one of them. Well, in any way other than the obvious.

Martin Salvi and Gabriel Wilcox became, overnight, just two guys jostling over position.

And I was determined that it would stop.

* * *

"I informed you I'd have your badge if you spoke to her alone," Martin said as he rushed through the door with a laser-focus on Gabe. "Just give me a reason, Wilcox."

"Oh, calm *down*, baby Capone," Gabe told him with a wave of his hand. The pithy name-calling seemed to enrage Martin, but Gabe continued before he could speak. "Don't storm in here like you own the place. You may run everything over at the compound, but—"

"You're putting her in jeopardy!" Martin informed him bitterly. "You know she's still a suspect, and you know she shouldn't be speaking to you without a lawyer!"

"Right, like *you* aren't putting her in danger?" Gabe responded coldly. "Just breathing around her is risky, Salvi. And you know it."

"Gentleman, could we tuck them back in our trousers and settle down?" I urged them as I stepped between their puffed out chests and physically forced them apart. "I don't want to fight with either of you, and this...*thing* between the two of you? It's an issue for me."

"Fortuna, I realize that you think I'm being possessive, but you don't know how crooked this police division is," Martin said furiously as he scowled at Gabe. "Incompetence is one thing, but I don't want you to get caught up in some frame job."

"And you *would* know about those, wouldn't you?" Gabe spat back. "First, I'm not *the police department*, I'm one man. And I care about Fortuna too much to let her get plowed under by the ineptitude that *you* support with your bribes and *contributions*."

"Oh, you care about her, do you? Is that why you keep talking to her without an attorney? Care about her so much that you've left her defenseless while talking to a cop?"

"Hey!" I protested, but they just argued over me.

"I'm not *just* a cop, I'm her friend! I don't have an agenda, like some people—"

"Oh, no?" Martin sneered. "You don't have an agenda like me? Really? Wilcox, I never pegged you for an unmitigated liar, but I suppose I was mistaken."

Gabe turned red.

"Enough!" I yelled, but that only caused the ill will to turn on me.

"The call that precipitated the raid on *your* shop came from his complex!" Gabriel said as he jabbed a finger in Martin's direction. "From his complex, while he had you eating fancy food in Little Rock!"

"So, you're criticizing me for something that happened at a place I manage when I *wasn't even there*, but it's *my* fault?" Martin asked Gabe. "What are you accusing me of, Wilcox?"

"We don't have time for me to list it all."

"This isn't helping," I told them both, glowering back and forth between them.

Martin broke out laughing. "You expected this would help?"

"Oh, lord, would you both just sit down over there?" I pointed to the seating area. They both regarded me and pondered whether to move. "I mean it! Go sit!"

Hesitantly, they finally wandered over and sat

down.

"Now, look," I said in as reassuring a tone as I could manage in an attempt to ratchet down the tension. Moving deliberately, I seated myself an equal distance between the two men. They had, of course, chosen chairs on contrary sides of the alcove. "This can't continue."

"I agree," Martin said. Gabriel rolled his eyes.

"You're both my friends," I told the two men as townspeople peeked into the shop and lifted (as well as lowered) eyebrows at the spectacle inside. Great. I'm sure the next rumor would be about some kind of love triangle...okay, well, maybe sometimes people's hunches weren't *altogether* off. "And I plan to continue a friendship with both of you. Neither one of you has screwed me over yet—that I know about."

I studied Martin Salvi pointedly.

"What?" he asked, confused.

"Yesterday, you came over and said that the report against me came from a phone call," I told him as Gabe turned to confront him, his eyes tightening. "How did you know that the tip was made by phone?"

"Yesterday morning, I overheard Joe Arturo and Angie Laroux talking in the hallway outside the Centre Club about the tip that had been called in," Martin told me, his hand rubbing his clean-shaven face. Within a few hours, I knew his face would be covered with a five o'clock shadow that gave him that smolderingly sexy bad boy air of mystery. "The hallway has some decorations that give two spots a whispering gallery effect. That is by design—it's so the guard in the front hallway can hear what's being said near the door at the end of the entryway."

"What time was this?" Gabriel asked him.

"Early in the morning. I'd say about nine."

"*That's* early in the morning to you?" Gabriel frowned.

"When you're not in bed by ten, choirboy, it—"

"Who's Joe Arturo?" I broke in and asked Martin before the two of them could start up anew.

"Joe Arturo owns the fancy hot dog stand at the track," Pepper said as she blew in to the store and looked at all of us. "He's also the business partner of Hugh Maddox."

The three of us stared at Pepper as she dropped her backpack and sat down without being invited.

* * *

"First of all, you should know that the word is you're polyandrous and seeing both of these guys with the intent on having a double wedding with two husbands," Pepper said as she hitched her thumb toward Martin and Gabriel. "I have to admit,

I'm impressed with the salaciousness of the story in such a limited time. The town's getting more original. And quicker."

"I'm *what* now?" We'd been in here collectively for twenty minutes. Tops.

"The next time you guys want to have a huge, dramatic fight where you step into the midst of them like it's a sexy bachelor sandwich with you as the cream filling, go into the back studio to do it."

I couldn't believe just how dirty Pepper made thirty seconds of an argument sound.

"So, here's the thing—he's not a part of the plot," she told me as she nodded toward Martin. "The trip to Little Rock was just a fluke. A weird one, sure, but I don't think he's part of whatever's going on with Hugh's death."

"Of course not!" Martin retorted, astonished. He swiveled around to look at me. "You worried I took you to Little Rock as part of some scheme?"

"Well, it was because—" I stopped and glanced at Gabriel.

"Don't," Pepper said under her breath.

She was right. We couldn't bring up the can of paint with Gabriel sitting here. They wouldn't be able to find it—I had used the cauldron to pass it to Charlotte in Mickwac for safe-keeping—but just informing him we hid evidence was...I mean, it was against the law. Technically.

"Don't what?" Gabe asked her, frowning.

"Look, handsome, you're a cop," Pepper said as she sagged back in the chair and flung her feet over the armrest. "I know it bugs you not to be told information, but your occupation was your choice, bud. Your department is trying to pin a murder on her. I'm working on dredging up information to help her. What are you doing?"

"I'm trying to help her—"

"If I told you I found evidence, would you be compelled to turn it over?" she challenged him, her chin set.

"Well, of course—"

"Yeah, so, we'll finish this discussion when he's left," Pepper told me as she dropped her chin and began fidgeting with the books on the end table next to her.

"Pepper," Detective Gabriel Wilcox said in his best cop voice. "If you have evidence of a crime, you *have* to turn it over."

"Do I?" she asked him, smirking. "Did I say I had evidence of a crime? I don't believe I said that I *am* in possession of evidence of a crime. I don't even think I said I *knew* of any evidence of a crime. I just asked a *theoretical* question, G. You answered the question. For now, we're done talking."

"Remember what I said about an attorney?" Martin asked me quietly. I turned to look at him.

He was staring at Pepper with something like admiration. "Maybe you *don't* need one."

"You're a sweetheart," Pepper beamed at him. "I do have a lawyer-like bulldogging tenacity about me, don't I? You may be the first person in this town that *likes* that about me." Pepper batted her eyes at him, and he chuckled.

"Pepper Stanford, what did you find?" Gabriel asked her again.

"I'm *not* kidding, Gabe," Pepper said as she turned back to him, her jovial demeanor turning serious. "You can't be a part of this conversation. I'm sorry."

A deep line emerged between Gabe's brows, and his eyes grew wide as he realized Pepper *really* would say nothing more while he was in the place. Seconds passed, and I could practically see his mind racing through for some rationale, some compelling argument about why she should.

But he couldn't find one.

"Gabriel, I *promise*, I'll watch out for her," Pepper told him genuinely, her eyes flicking over to me. Turning back, their gazes met. "But you *have* to go. Quit your job, or go. You can't straddle a line here. Not with so much at stake for Fortuna."

Gabriel stood up, scowling at Martin.

Then he turned on his heel and stormed out.

NINE

"It's that he likes you," Pepper said as we sat in the back of Martin's limo. "Gabe always gets like this with women he likes. Are you *sure* he hasn't asked you out on a date?"

"I'm sure he hasn't asked me out on a date," I told her as Martin looked out the window pretending not to listen to the conversation. "He's said nothing romantic of the sort. Miss Bessie, on the other hand, demands that I marry him pronto and start popping out grandchildren."

Pepper chuckled. "That woman's a spitfire."

"I still don't understand what you're hoping to find out from Angie," Martin said as he turned back toward Pepper. "That, and I don't know that bringing Fortuna with you will go over very well."

"Why, because Angie wants you and you want her?" Pepper asked cheerfully. "Anyway, I'm hoping Fortuna will rattle her a little. Knock her off her game. Maybe she'll tell the truth by accident."

"You don't pull any punches, do you, dear?" Martin asked as he stared at her, amused.

"Pulled punches don't *land*, Marty," Pepper responded. Martin frowned at the nickname. "What's the matter, don't enjoy being called Marty?" Pepper's eyes lit up as she smelled a story behind the frown.

"I just *prefer* Martin, thank you," he answered formally, and then shifted in his seat. "It's just a matter of taste."

"You don't like to *shorten* names? *Never?*" Pepper asked him suspiciously. Martin stared daggers at her, and now *I* was detecting a tale behind the glare.

"Do you want to get out and walk, Ms. Stanford?" Martin asked her coldly. I looked back and forth between the two of them. The sudden tension was thicker than the goop that made the communication cauldron work.

"The half-mile to the door? Sure!" she answered cheerfully as she looked out the window. "You want to have your servant stop the car, or are you going to just push me out while it's rolling?"

Martin's eyes narrowed dangerously, but he didn't respond.

"What's going on?" I asked them both.

No one answered.

"We're here, Mr. Salvi," the driver announced as he pulled up in front of the Mystic's End complex. "Do you wish me to call—"

"No, Jeeves, that's fine," Martin told him, and my jaw dropped.

"Your driver's name is Jeeves?"

"No, it's Chris, actually," Martin half-smiled as he waited for the driver to come and open the door. "I liked the Wodehouse books, so I call him Jeeves. Once he read them, he didn't mind as much."

The three of us climbed out of the limo, and three people ran up to him with clipboards and grievances as soon as his feet hit the road. Martin glanced over, held up a finger, and walked off to handle whatever work crisis needed his attention.

"Hey, what was all that in the car?" I asked Pepper after pulling her behind the vehicle, my voice low.

"How much has he told you about his family, where he comes from?" Pepper asked me as her eyes followed Martin. Her voice was low, almost a whisper—which was surprising. I didn't think Pepper had a volume below *booming*.

"Not much, really," I told her, shrugging. "I

know he was born in Las Vegas, he went to school in California. Stanford, I think." I squinted into the afternoon sun, thinking. "Honestly, we don't talk about our past a lot. Mostly, we've kept it light. You know, dinner talk. Talk about the businesses, the town. Not a lot of deep dives."

"Maybe you should," she said, her eyes still watching Martin.

"Pepper, what is it you know that I don't?"

"Well, a lot, actually," she acknowledged as she shifted back to me. "But about Martin? Nothing for sure. Which is why I haven't said anything. You two have been friends, and he seems like an okay enough guy. Honestly, for all the rumors about him being mobbed up, I've never been able to find a single thing on the guy. But that's just it."

"What's it?"

"I've never been able to find a *single thing* on the guy," she told me. "He doesn't *exist* before he moved here and became the overseer of this whole place. No one named Martin Salvi was born in Vegas in 1979. No one named Martin Salvi graduated from Stanford. It's like the guy popped out of nowhere to run this place."

I turned and glanced at Martin. Almost as if he felt my eyes on him, he turned and smiled warmly at me.

"I don't like things I can't explain," Pepper

sighed. "And I can't explain him. He's either too good to be true—handsome, rich, successful, *and* single—or *highly* skilled at being bad."

* * *

"Martin, to what do we, ah, owe the pleasure of your visit?" Evangeline Laroux purred as Martin walked into the Centre Supper Club. Employees ran around frantically setting tables with fancy porcelain plates and crystal wine glasses. "Did you come to—oh, it's *you*," Angie deadpanned as the kitten purr left her voice the moment she spotted me.

"Angie, Pepper has some questions about your discussion with Joe Arturo yesterday," Martin said as we stepped up next to her. Angie was sitting down at a linen-covered table, a wine glass next to her. Several bottles were nearby. "And I want to know why you called to report Fortuna to the police."

"Why, Martin," she said, purring again as she snaked her hand to his waist and clutched his hip. "If you want to know, I'd be more than willin' to go someplace private, away from all these prying eyes, and," Angie hesitated, her smoldering eyes half closing as she looked up at him and licked her lips, "talk."

Martin grabbed her hand gently and removed it. Then he took two steps back.

"Well, now, you are just no fun, Martin," Angie said as she wobbled in his direction. The woman leaned over to ensure that her substantial cleavage was precisely in Martin's sight line. There was a greedy hunger in her smoldering sensuality that was practically indecent to watch. I glanced away.

"Look, Clutterbuck, I can guess why you called the cops on Fortuna. One, she figured out you and your high school boy toy killed someone in her house," Pepper said as her annoyance flared. "What I can't understand is how you knew conductive paint killed Hugh Maddox before anyone else."

"*Don't* call me that," Angie Laroux (formerly Rowena Clutterbuck) hissed as she stood up only to stumble drunkenly on her heels. Martin reached out to steady her, and as soon as he touched her, she melted back into a sex kitten and giggled at him as she fluttered her eyes.

"Dear lord, woman, you need therapy," I said out loud. Accidentally. Maybe.

"You shut up," she turned and hissed at me. "My life was just *fine* before you showed up here. Now people *stare* at me."

"I got news for you, Evangeline, I have a feeling they were staring at you before," I told her as I gestured to the clingy, almost translucent dress that showed off every curve she had.

"Witch!" she said, trembling with fury.

Pepper chuckled.

"Why would you call the anonymous tip line to report whatever you were reporting, anyway?" I asked her. "Your father is the Chief of Police. Why not just call *him* and tell him what you know?"

"If I told Daddy, then people would *know* I reported it, you moron," Evangeline told me drunkenly. "This way, *no* one knew it was me that turned you in!" She laughed triumphantly.

"See what I mean? The gates are down and the lights are flashing, but the train's not coming," Pepper told Martin. "Though, honestly, as drunk as she is? We might have been able to accomplish this with a phone call."

"I'm not drunk!" she screamed at Pepper. The force of the shout rocked her unsteadily on her six-inch heels. It was only Martin's hand on her arm keeping her upright.

"Of course not," Pepper smirked, glancing at the two empty liquor bottles on the table.

"I don't like you," Evangeline slurred as she leaned toward me with an unsteady lurch. "You stole Martin from me, and I don't like you." Martin remained mute as he gawked at Evangeline with sympathy. "But I don't fault you for killin' that stupid Hugh Maddox."

"I didn't—"

"You don't," Pepper told her as she cut off my denial. "I mean, that's obvious. How could *anyone* blame Fortuna for killing that man?"

"Right?" she replied, her voice high pitched.

"All those things he did, all the sins he committed. All those years of...ugh. Surely *someone* would do it eventually." Martin was looking at Pepper with his jaw slightly open.

"I thought he would leave Della, but no," Angie shook her head violently. "No, he just told me he would over and over again. He couldn't even buy me very expensive presents, either. Because Della would see that the money was missing," Angie declared, red-faced, and then squeezed her eyes shut. "I waited, and waited, and waited—three whole months!"

"Three months?" Pepper gasped with feigned shock. "You had a relationship with him for *three entire months*, and he never left his wife? Unbelievable!"

"I know, *right*?" She opened her eyes, and they shot sparks as she swayed on her feet. "Three months, and nothing but a few rings and a diamond pendant. The nerve of that man!"

"That must have been difficult for you," I murmured.

"You *shut* up," she spat, spinning on me unsteadily. "Joe *told* me at the party you were seeing him, too. That's when I *knew* you had killed him," she shrieked. "But that's not why I'm mad. I mean, trying to get him and trying to get Martin? You have a lot of nerve! This is *my* town!"

It astonished me she still looked amazing even as she had a drunken meltdown. She also looked amazing as she leaped at me, but she was so slow and so drunk that I stepped out of the way easily.

"I hate you, Fortuna! I hate you!" she wailed as her employees came running. She writhed in Martin's grip and varied between wiggling against him and struggling to grab me.

"I think we got what we needed," Pepper nodded at Martin. He nodded once back and jerked his head toward the door, signaling that we should leave.

"I'll get you, Fortuna Delphi!" Evangeline shouted after me as Pepper and I walked coolly out the door. "I'll get you if it's the last thing I do!"

* * *

"So, I don't think she likes you," Pepper said as we lingered at the end of the long passageway to the Club.

"Gee, you think?" I responded sarcastically.

"I wouldn't worry about it too much. She's got all she can handle just trying to walk and talk at the same time," Pepper observed as she leaned against the wall. "I think we can cross her off the list of suspects. This took planning skills that woman *clearly* doesn't possess. At least not in her current state."

"So, Joe Arturo, Hugh's business partner, informed her that Hugh and I were having an affair. Why would he tell her that?" I asked Pepper.

"That she wants Martin Salvi, and that Martin Salvi wants you? These aren't *exactly* secrets in Mystic's End, Fortuna," Pepper said. "It wouldn't take a genius to put two and two together. Maybe Joe realized that he could spin her into a tizzy, and she would act on it."

"Why would he need to? And *she's* a jilted ex-mistress. Why would Angie put herself on the radar like that?" I pointed out. "Joe may have said *I* was having an affair with Hugh, but I wasn't. She was."

"Maybe she's the fall back suspect? If blaming you doesn't work out?"

"It tracks," I sighed. "The paint was planted on me. They made sure she learned about it before the police did. So, they could view either of us a suspect if you look at it a certain way. So, we think Joe did it, then?"

"We have to find out who planted that paint," Pepper said as she shoved herself off the wall and squinted out into the courtyard in front of the corridor. "I don't know how, though. The only witness to it was your dog. And he's not saying any more than he has."

"Joe Arturo," I told her, nodding. "That's the only lead we have. Wait a minute." I said, an idea suddenly occurring to me. "What about the guys that picked up the statue?"

"What about them?"

"What if they didn't take it straight to the Maddox house? There wasn't *any* paint on the dais. It *had* to have been painted somewhere else—that job was clumsy." I shivered, remembering the pooled globs of paint on my lovely angel.

"Do you know who they are?"

"They left a copy of the pickup sheet," I told her. She nodded. I looked at my watch and noticed it was past noon. "I have to go back to the shop, anyway. I need to get the painting over to the church in time for the funeral."

"Okay, we'll ask Martin and his luxury barge to drop us off. Unless he's coming with us," Pepper said as she looked at me.

"I'm not sure what his plans are."

"Really? Because I have to tell you, they seem *pretty* darn clear to me," Pepper chuckled and raised an eyebrow. "What's your deal with him? You spend a lot of time together. He's smoking hot. Aside from that whole *who the hell is he and where does he come from* thing, he's practically perfect."

"Until yesterday, I wasn't sure if I was related to him," I told her as I sat down on a bench near the entrance. "When Miss Bessie told me I wasn't, it was a relief, but it also puts me in a position of having choices." I paused. "I think I liked it better when I didn't, to tell you the truth."

"And you say *I'm* strange," Pepper rolled her eyes.

"I like him."

"So go out with him."

"I don't know him well enough."

"So *get* to know him," Pepper said with a hint of irritation.

"I *am* getting to know him!"

"Are you?"

Pepper had an ability to strip away all the protections around the truth being hidden. Sometimes, it was annoying. Sometimes, it was needed.

"Look, I'm not feeling...secure here yet," I admitted to her. Pepper stared at me intently, her eyes glinting with sympathy. "I never felt rooted with my adoptive family. The circus was as much of a home as I ever felt I had, but even that disappeared into a puff of smoke at the end. It's not...easy for me to trust things. Or people."

"Fair enough," Pepper nodded. "But maybe you should start doing some of that deep diving stuff and *tell* him that."

"Maybe."

"Or you could always just marry Gabe," Pepper joked as she elbowed me. "Miss Bessie would throw the biggest party the old folks' home has ever seen." Though she laughed, I could see a flicker of pain pass over her eyes.

"You still care about him," I said quietly to her.

"I told you I do," she shrugged and looked away. "I *always* will. It doesn't mean that he'll *ever* pull that stick out of his butt and walk on the wild side with me. Gabe will always see me as something to *manage*. And that's not a life I can live."

I grabbed her hand and squeezed it, and we sat quietly on the bench waiting for Martin.

Neither one of us remembered that the corridor was a whispering room, and we had no idea Martin had stood outside the doors of the Club listening to every word we said.

TEN

"What is this?" I asked as I trudged up to the shop door and spied an envelope fastened to the front. Tearing the pouch off, I pulled out papers. "I don't understand this."

"What is it?" Martin asked.

"They ruled the death accidental," I told him, glancing up.

"That's great, right?" Pepper asked as she stepped toward me to look through the papers over my shoulder.

"You'd think. But they're blaming me, anyway." I passed the papers to her and took out my keys to unlock the door. "There's a hearing two days from now on pulling my occupancy permit."

"They want to shut down the gallery?" Martin asked, frowning. Pepper held up a finger as she tore through the bundle of papers.

"And evict her. They're saying she was negligent. That Hugh's death was an accident, but it was because of the business's negligence with the statue that he's dead," Pepper frowned as she scoured.

"So, the good news is I will not go to jail, but the bad news is they will run me out of town on a rail," I sighed as I stepped in. Gideon ran up to me and nuzzled my hand.

"Will you *listen* to me now and get an attorney?" Martin asked me as he walked over and put his hands on my arms. I tensed from his touch and he dropped his hands, his face worried. "They're clearly fixated on you for this, and they're working to blame you any way they can."

"Yeah, but *why?*" Pepper asked, glowering, and then turned to Martin. "Okay, Salvi, look. Let's you and I call a truce on the whole *I think you're super corrupt* thing for a minute. I will set aside my distrust of you, and anything you say here will be off the record."

Martin frowned. "Okay."

"Why are they going after her so hard?"

"How would I know?" Martin asked her. "It's not like I have the chief of police on speed dial."

"Oh, come on. Don't you?"

Martin shifted uneasily and dropped his eyes for a second. Looking back up, he nodded. "Yes, okay, I do, but he and I aren't *friends*. We don't golf or go out and have drinks. We discuss things that relate to the complex, but I have little insight into what goes on in the town beyond what affects my— my organization."

"Bull," Pepper shot back.

"Look, I *know* what you think of me," Martin shot back sharply in an uncanny echo of what Pepper had said to me earlier. Gideon turned his head toward Martin and angled it sideways, as if Martin's defensive anger surprised him. "I know what *everybody* in this town thinks of me."

Martin whirled on his heel and faced the front window, his remote gaze scanning over the street but seeing nothing. "I assumed I could avoid it here, but I never will, will I?" he mumbled to himself.

What the heck?

"Avoid what?" I said as I walked over to him and reached out my hand to his shoulder. When I did, the turbulence, hopelessness, and resentment that was psychically leaking from him nearly rocked me off my feet. I tried to steady myself and stared up at him. "Martin...avoid what?"

"I'm sorry," he declared as he turned to me, his eyes clearing and his face growing stoic. "That was uncalled for." His voice was clearing, becoming stronger. I felt the undercurrent of emotions within him retreat.

"There's no need to apolo—"

"I can help you by hiring you an attorney to represent you. No more of this defensive rejection of my help, Fortuna. Look at it as one business helping another. That's all."

Well, I guess we weren't going to talk about that anymore.

I let him drop it, for now.

I thought about protesting against his offer again, but Martin was right. I *didn't* have a business attorney here, and he likely had a phalanx of the best lawyers in the state on staff at the complex. Finally, I nodded. "But *I* pay for it. I'll take your advice because you know more about this than I do, but *I* pay my way, Martin. That's non-negotiable."

He smiled and nodded, drawing his cell phone from his pocket and walking out the door to make the call.

"What the heck was *that* about?" Pepper asked as we watched Martin, back in command, bark orders at someone through the phone.

"You accused him of being corrupt to his face?" I suggested. "People that aren't corrupt don't tend to like that much. Maybe that's all it was."

"Yeah, but...that wasn't it. That was something

else. Even *I* could feel that, and I don't have any powers at all other than observation," she told me softly. "There's something going on with him."

I didn't respond.

* * *

"Gerard Blatworth, ma'am," a sophisticated, dark-haired man said as he held out an impeccably manicured hand for me to shake. "Mr. Salvi has advised me of the situation, and with your consent, I will represent you in this matter."

"Nice to meet you, Mr. Blatworth," I nodded. "I appreciate you taking the time out to help me on what, to you, must seem like a small matter. It's important to me."

"Quite," he said as he snapped at the four men trailing him and pointed toward the back.

"Who are they?" I asked, frowning.

"The other attor—"

"Mr. Blatworth's associates," Martin cut him off and gave the man a fierce look. "They're included in the price you'll be paying for Mr. Blatworth's time."

"Uh huh," I asked skeptically, my eyes narrowing. "And what *is* that price, exactly?" Judging by Blatworth's suit, I could afford *maybe* three threads worth of time after paying fifty-thousand for Gideon.

"Lucky for you, Ms. Delphi, that we have not met our pro bono quota for the month, so our services will come at no cost to you. I assume those are the county's papers?" Mr. Blatworth asked, pointing to the papers in my hands. I gave them to him.

"If someone *were* paying you, you'd *have* to tell me, right? Since I'm your client and not, say, a tall, dark, and handsome gentleman?" Pepper silently watched from the side of the room.

"You think I'm handsome?" Martin inquired, grinning wickedly.

"I can assure you, Ms. Delphi, you will get nothing but honesty from us, as I hope we will get from you," Mr. Blatworth nodded. He nodded cordially to his employer and then turned to join his fellow attorneys in my workshop. I turned toward Martin.

"What?"

"I feel like this pushes the bounds of the spirit of our agreement, here, Salvi. They just so happen to have pro bono hours they need to perform? Really," I told him, crossing my arms. His eyes gleamed and the bemused expression was back.

"Can a spirit *truly* have boundaries?"

"Spike would absolutely think so," Pepper

muttered. I scowled at her. "What? What'd I say?" I shot my eyes over to Martin, and then back to her, wide. I considered trying to shove that Martin didn't *know* I could see ghosts straight into her brain, but I abstained because of my newly adopted and altogether inconvenient sense of principles.

Even though Pepper and her loose mouth totally deserved it.

"Oh, right, he doesn't know," she shrugged. "Sorry. I forgot."

"I don't know what?" Martin asked, his eyes moving back and forth between me and Pepper. "Something I should know?"

I could kill Pepper sometimes.

"Hey, I have a suggestion! *You* tell her what you were talking about a minute ago, you know, about the thing you can't avoid," Pepper said nodding to Martin. "She'll tell you what *I'm* talking about. Then everybody gets what they want and we all learn something about each other. Deal?"

Martin laughed as if it were a joke, trailing off once he realized Pepper Stanford was sincere. The giveaway was how she peered at him, pen poised in her pad, watching impatiently.

Martin's eyes drifted to me, and we stared at one another, both of our expressions as inscrutable as we could make them. His eyes, though, were laden with curiosity and shadows as they searched mine. Finally, he smiled at me.

"Perhaps everyone needs some secrets," he announced.

"I guess so," I concurred.

* * *

"There looks to be no evidence here that gives the county or city the right to pull your certificate of occupancy, or C of O, based solely on what transpired with Mr. Maddox," Mr. Blatworth announced an hour later after the attorneys had made some phone calls and discussed my situation. "The C of O simply says the building is safe or not safe, and what is in it. I don't see how they can justify pulling it based on a faulty product sale, and why that is cited here, I do not understand." The other lawyers nodded.

"That's good, right?" I said, sighing with relief.

"Not entirely," Mr. Blatworth replied.

"What do you mean?"

"It appears they are doing an end run to get you out with a valid claim," Mr. Blatworth explained. "While there are pages about Mr. Maddox and his demise, the last line is the only line that needed to be introduced."

"And that last line is?" Martin asked.

"That this is a commercial building, not a residence," the lawyer to the right of Mr. Blatworth stated. Blatworth nodded in agreement. "They issued you a C of O for the gallery, not for the residence upstairs. While there is a notation on your C of O at the bottom that there *is* an apartment, the notation is not, strictly speaking, valid."

"But the inspector said that was what I needed, I paid him, and we were done," I frowned. "How was I supposed to know the notation made the certificate invalid?"

The five attorneys smiled at one another and nodded knowingly. "That's why you have us, dear," Blatworth said, and I cringed at a man only slightly older than me addressing me with a phrase that I'd hoped had been retired long ago. It made me feel like a child. "Who represented you for the purchase and rehab of this building? He or she never should have let this go through."

"My name is Ms. Delphi," I told him. "As to your question, well, I mean...I did, I guess. The real estate agent suggested the folks I needed to contact for the permits and so on, and I just—"

I stopped talking while the five lawyers tsk-tsked my ignorance and shook their heads, murmuring to one another about the scarcity of attorneys involved and how all of this could have been averted. My eyes narrowed and I bristled at the murmuring.

They continued, ignoring my expression. Just as I was about to say something, a stern look from Martin stopped the men cold.

"Man, I hate lawyers," Pepper muttered.

"I don't think it's a lawyer thing, I think it's a man thing," I muttered back.

Clearing his throat, Blatworth continued. "We will each work on different aspects of the case, and surely we can straighten out the situation before the hearing in two days. Our goal is not only to avoid the hearing but to have the proper C of O in your hands before twenty-four hours is up."

"That fast?"

"We're very good at what we do, dear—um, Ms. Delphi," Blatworth said, smiling up at me. Gideon stuck his head under the man's arm and looked up at him. Blatworth jumped. "Oh my. There looks to be a dog in here," he added disdainfully.

"Gideon," I called, and the dog sighed loudly, snaking back out from Blatworth's lap and walking over to me. "Sorry about that."

"Quite," he responded as he picked greyhound hairs off his extremely expensive suit one by one, grimacing.

* * *

"I *have* to get this portrait to the church," I told Pepper as Martin spoke quietly to the attorneys gathered by the door.

"Can he take you?" Pepper gestured toward Martin.

"You know, I *have* a car," I quipped as I bundled up the painting to protect it on the ride over. "I can even drive *all by myself*, too. Not that the testosterone brigade over there would believe it."

"So, don't take my feminist card for saying this, but I don't want you going over there alone," Pepper told me privately with her back to the six men at the front. "This all sounds so...targeted. *Someone* doesn't want you here, and frankly, I'm wondering how deep that goes."

"You're being absurd," I waved off her worry. "The only reason they looked at me was because Susie Sexpot saw a way to push me out so she could take another run at Martin. It wouldn't surprise me in the least bit if this was all just more of the same."

"Well, that, and your statue *killed* a man," Pepper reminded me. "Let's not ignore how this all started, Fortuna. Maddox is dead, and whatever that stupid paper says, that's *no* accident. There's too much hinky about this whole event, and Evangeline Laroux doesn't strike me as a criminal mastermind. My conspiracy radar is screaming... hey, don't give me that look."

"I'm not giving you *any* look. You're paranoid."

Okay, I was giving her a bit of a look.

"I *am* paranoid, but you totally gave me a look."

Maybe I had grown so used to being targeted at the Magical Midway that what was roiling around me just didn't seem all that big of a deal. It worried me, sure. But if you contrast a yanked certificate of occupancy with getting lightning bolts hurled at you by a god?

There was no contest.

I could deal with attacks by paperwork.

"Okay, look, I don't mean to suggest I'm not taking this seriously," I answered as I sat down on the stool behind the counter. "You're right, it looks to me like Hugh Maddox is dead because someone wanted him that way. Whoever did it assumed the police would know that because they went to the trouble of planting the silver paint to throw off the scent."

"I sincerely don't know why. I told you before, there's always some innocuous explanation for catastrophes in Mystic's End."

"Maybe they were just covering their bases? Who knows?"

"*I* want to know," Pepper said as she put her notebook and pen in her backpack and then slung it on her back. "I'm going to go over to the hall of records before it closes and get a copy of the death certificate."

"A death certificate this quickly?" I asked dumbfounded.

"Haven't you learned yet? No one in this town does any actual work when it comes to law enforcement," Pepper smirked. "That means the case is closed before the body is cold. Besides, I bet Della was up their butts asking for it so she could get whatever enormous insurance policy she doubtless had on Hugh to pay out. While I'm there, I'll see if I can check that out, too."

"How?"

"I'll tell you later," Pepper said as she spotted Martin walking back over to us. "Trade secrets and all."

"Right."

"We'll meet back here at six to go to the funeral?" Pepper asked as she shoved back off the counter and stood up. I nodded. Turning to Martin, she added, "Don't take your eyes off her. I don't totally trust you're not crooked, but you're the only guy I know with an armed guard at all times, so—

"Wait, what?" I asked, taken aback.

"Toodles, folks!" Pepper said as she strolled toward the door.

ELEVEN

"I feel like I should apologize for the hostility with Gabriel," Martin said as his driver took us toward the Holy Grove Church.

I glanced over at Martin with curiosity. This was the thing on his mind as we left the gallery after the attorneys decamped to save my business?

Sure, okay, let's talk about *Gabe*.

"When I first got here and Gideon kept showing up on my doorstep, Gabriel seemed skittish about bringing the dog back," I said, turning to him. "He said something about people at the track possibly accusing him of stealing the dog or something."

"I don't know that I would say the dislike goes

that far," Martin answered with an inelegant snort. "But yes, there's some history there."

"Such as?"

"Such as Gabriel seems to believe the track is a front for something. Drugs, maybe. Human trafficking? Money laundering? I don't know, really, but he tried to investigate two years ago, and he was...*indelicate* in his indictments," Martin told me. Martin's expression didn't indicate Gabriel's attempt to unmask the complex as a criminal organization especially irked him. "Some people took offense."

"You?"

"Not particularly," Martin shrugged, turning to watch my reaction with an amused glint in his eye. "Don't get me wrong, I don't enjoy taking time out of my day to deal with a search warrant. A situation you, sadly, now have first-hand experience with."

"Gabe served search warrants on you?"

"The complex, yes. Not me *individually*. My father was not pleased."

"Your father?"

Martin paused and I waited.

"In any case," he said, neglecting my question, "Gabe made more work for those at the track, so he's not the most popular person there. It also forced many of the workers to be on their toes, and they didn't like that very much, either."

"You're talking about this situation like it didn't affect the relationship between you and Gabe much at all. Well, I mean...did the two of you even know each other before that? Is that whole thing why you don't like him?"

"I like him just fine."

"Hard to believe. No offense."

"Gabriel has a very precise view regarding who is expected to eat discomfort, and who may force-feed it to others," Martin replied as we drew into the church parking lot. "It annoys me, I'll grant. I loathe the hubris that can be tucked away behind a badge."

"Martin, you have to recognize that sounds ridiculous coming from you," I told him, inclining my head. "You strut around like you own the place even when you don't."

"Confidence *isn't* hubris, and my confidence comes from who I *am*, not a badge of authority or..." he trailed off as the door opened. "Look, I don't hide behind anything or anyone. I am just me, Fortuna. I dislike people that force control they haven't earned."

We looked at each other for a few moments, and despite Martin's statement, I felt he had crossed boundaries with me he hadn't earned. I said as much, and to that, he grinned broadly.

"First, I have paid in shrimp scampi so I can

have *some* presumption and feel good about it,"
Martin said with a smile, his index finger raised.
"Second, I hope that I have earned, at least, the
right to be in your life and convey my concern for
you."

"You know, even if I *could* be bought, shrimp
scampi is a pretty cheap price," I told him. "It
would have to be—"

"Third," he went on, his face turning serious, "I
don't think romantic relationships are a matter of
earning chits for favors. I want you to listen to me
because you expect I care for you and have your
best interests at heart."

"You don't think Gabe has my best interests at
heart?"

"*He* served you with a warrant. *I* helped you get
attorneys," Martin answered as he turned to get out
of the limo. "I suspect our actions speak louder than
our words do, Fortuna. In the end, it's for you to
decide."

* * *

Martin's driver carefully brought the painting
into the church. It wasn't a large church,
but it wasn't small, either. A large rectangle brick
and stone structure with an odd square tower on the
southwest corner, the bricks a bright gray-white.

The doors to enter the Late Gothic style church were directly under the threatening-looking tower.

"How old is this place?" I asked Martin as I peered at the sinister looking stained-glass windows. Despite the bright white facade, the church was nevertheless as dark and bleak as I remembered it. "When Spike's funeral was here I recall being struck by how old it looked."

"It's right around a hundred years old, I think," Martin said as he pointed his driver to the easel on the dais. "There's a plaque on the front that gives a bit of information, if you're interested."

"It's just so...creepy," I shivered as we continued to move toward the front.

"Perhaps it's the divine energy you feel pressing down on you, the celestial presence urging you to stop your wicked ways," Dexter Kane said as he strode out from a side door. He smiled until he spotted Martin Salvi and the feigned smile dropped into a frown. "Martin, I didn't expect to see you here."

"I've been helping Fortuna with...the situation," Martin responded without elaborating.

"Have you now?" the clergyman deadpanned.

"Since she's new in town, I thought I could help her navigate. Considering I've been in a similar dilemma before," Martin responded. I glanced back and forth between the two men wondering where on *earth* the unease between them came from. I'd seen them together already, and they *looked* friendly.

"We just came by to make sure the painting got here before the people did, Reverend," I said as I gestured toward Hugh Maddox's portrait. "I hope that Mrs. Maddox likes it."

"Yes, yes, I'm sure she will," he acknowledged without turning to look at it. He locked his eyes on Martin Salvi. "Tell me, Martin, are you aware that this woman used to be a fortune teller? I wouldn't expect your father would—"

"My father has no influence on who I have as a friend, Reverend Kane," Martin spat back. His eyes narrowed dangerously, and the arrogance—um, confidence—had creeped back into his manner. "And I have no tolerance for anyone who brings up my father in conversation to castigate me like an adolescent."

"Now, Martin—"

"Incidentally," Martin said after dropping his voice to a loud, exaggerated whisper, "my father doesn't much like it, either."

Martin had said surprisingly little to me about his family in Las Vegas, though I had shared an equal amount about my adoptive family—which is to say not a whole lot. I realized he was brought up by a family of means—we tend to be able to recognize one another (whether or not we want to). But he never discussed them beyond benign anecdotes and non-identifiable generic stories.

"Yes, of course, Mr. Salvi," Kane coughed, his eyes shifting. "Please excuse me, I meant no disrespect."

I arched a brow as I gawked at him. I'd never seen Kane humble. Ever. And the quick switcheroo to Martin's more formal greeting didn't pass unnoticed.

"Will you be attending the service?" Kane asked me respectfully.

"Yes, of course," I nodded. "I didn't know Mr. Maddox that well, but we had worked together on the statue."

"Yes, paradoxical, that, isn't it?" the reverend murmured. "That Hugh would be so *delighted* by the very thing that killed him in the end. Things we enjoy, that we think give us pleasure in life, those things can come back to make us pay, can't they?"

I had no idea what the heck this guy was talking about.

"The symbolism of an angel, too, a gift for Della being the very thing that ripped his life from his body," Kane said, his eyes becoming glassy as he waxed on. "I imagine Della is both grieved *and* triumphant that it proved her right."

"I'm sorry? *What* proved her right?" I asked.

"She told Hugh that his womanizing would cost him everything and would be his undoing if he didn't stop," Dexter replied, his eyes clearing as he looked down at me. "She knew if she just had faith in the almighty, she would be rewarded for not leaving him. And so she *has* been, no?"

The man's vengeful view of an unexpected death as payback was even creepier than his dark, gloomy chapel.

"You think some preterhuman power *killed* Hugh Maddox because he cheated on his wife?"

"I have to admit I find it odd that the man in charge would move through *you*," Reverend Kane said with scarcely concealed disdain. "But you are getting your own form of comeuppance, no? *You* are being brought quite low in this—"

"That's enough," Martin snapped as he stepped closer to me as if sensing menace from the clergyman. "They ruled the death an accident—"

"*Nothing* is an accident," Reverend Kane countered as he peered down at me. "Just ask Satan's mistress over there. The serpent with the pearl."

I gaped at the man as he stared.

* * *

"Has anyone taken Kane to see a psychiatrist?" I asked Martin as we left the Holy Grove Church. "Because I swear, that guy is a few screws *short* of a hardware store." The silent driver opened the door for us and nodded once. "And does he ever talk?" I asked, pointing to the driver. "Because I *don't* think he ever talks."

I clambered in to the cavernous limousine and struggled not to burst in fury. *Satan's mistress?* What kind of garbage was this? First, he hits on me like some lecherous sleazeball, then when I hand over the stupid painting he enlisted me to do, he doesn't even look at it—and throws me some theological lecture about my deserved punishment for...what?

I didn't cheat on anyone.

And I didn't put the stupid silver paint on the stupid angel!

If the stupid paint *really* electrocuted him.

Which I wasn't convinced of.

"He talks," Martin assured me as the car pulled away from ye old creepy church. "When it's needed. Hey," Martin said as he turned to me, his face growing concerned. "Are you okay? That crazy preacher's ramblings didn't bother you, did they? He's just a zealous nutcase, Fortuna. Ignore him."

"What is with this *stupid town?*" I exploded at him. "Pepper's right, this whole place is just *nuts!*

Why did I even *come* here?" I looked out the window, fuming.

I knew why I came here—no one but Pepper and Miss Bessie knew. Since I wasn't ready to hear why, exactly, I'd been dropped on steps in the town square and abandoned like yesterday's trash, *maybe* moving here was a mistake.

Maybe I should have stayed in Mickwac.

It was certainly starting to *feel* like a mistake.

"Why *did* you come here?" Martin asked me patiently.

"I came here to—" I stopped myself before I spilled my entire back story. His eyes were soft, and when they met mine, I felt the warmth in them. I turned, breaking the connection. "Forget it. Never mind."

"Fortuna—"

"I don't want to talk about it."

We drove silently, but I could feel his eyes on me, thinking.

"Fortuna—"

"I *said* I don't want to talk *about* it."

"Wow," Martin chuckled as he exhaled noisily. "You can be a hard woman, you know that? You don't even know what I was going to say."

Fat chance of that. I'm a mind reader, bub.

Only, of course, I *wasn't* at that moment. Avalon Grove's ethical lessons were things I was *trying* to adhere to, though this town was making it *more and more difficult* to refrain from peeling people's heads open like an onion.

Metaphorically, I mean.

"I'm sorry, what is it?" I said clearly, turning to look at him. My breath caught at his expression—gentle, soft, concerned. Loving. Martin Salvi really, *really* was *incredibly* handsome, and for a moment, attraction washed over me like a wave.

But I pushed it away.

"I'm sorry," Martin said simply, his exceptionally handsome face sympathetic, but not inordinately so. His eyes were piercing, and my breath caught again.

"What are *you* sorry for?" I asked him as I tried to cover the fact that in my weakened state, attraction to him was playing havoc with my insides.

Snippiness seemed effective for that.

"You looked so happy at the party, like you finally felt like you belonged in Mystic's End," Martin told me. I could tell he was being careful not to move forward toward me, not to violate my space. "I know that feeling, I guess. I'm...I'm disappointed that you don't seem to feel that way any longer. And I'm sorry for the things that took that from you."

For a moment, a flash leaked through my

careful shielding, and I could see within Martin, see through his eyes how *I* looked to him. He saw someone that might accept him, might understand *his* secrets—if only he could trust someone enough to speak them.

Martin thought we might, just *might*, be kindred spirits. That the *someone* he longed for might very well be me.

As we got out of the car and walked toward the shop, I wondered which one of us, if either, would speak of our secrets first.

And what would result when we did.

TWELVE

"How did you get in here?" I asked Pepper as I went in the front door to my shop. She was done up in mourning black from head to toe, her long, dark blonde hair pulled back into a conservative bun.

"The door clicked when I came up to it," she shrugged, not glancing up from the notebook she was looking through. "I figured Spike unlocked it or something, but it's not like I could see him when he did. You should go change so we can get to the funeral."

"Who's Spike?" Martin asked Pepper. Her head jerked up.

"Hey, Salvi, didn't realize you were here."

"Hello again, Pepper. Who's Spike?" he

inquired again as he moved toward the spot next to her and sat down. Her eyes darted over to me and I glared at her. If she had just *looked up* before she ran her mouth she could have dodged the question. Pepper raised an eyebrow, and I shook my head slightly.

"I saw that, Fortuna," Martin said without turning toward me. "My peripheral eyesight is extraordinarily good, you know."

"Ha ha, hilarious," I said as I spun and raced toward the back. "Look, I have to get changed for the funeral and feed Gideon," I said as I kept going. From somewhere upstairs, Gideon barked. "You two hang out down here, and I'll be back soon."

"Okay!" Martin called. Then I heard him ask again. "So, Pepper...who's Spike?"

* * *

"Aren't you excited that I can move things?" Spike asked as he flitted excitedly around my bedroom. "Watch!" The ghost halted his celebratory ping-ping and stared at a perfume bottle on my makeup desk. With a flash of blue light, the glass bottle shot off the desk and onto the floor, shattering into pieces. The entire room smelled like a bordello.

"That *would* have been notable if it didn't cost

me over a hundred dollars to witness," I told him with a grimace. "Where on earth have you been?"

"Well, I went to visit my dad," he said, and shivered. "Talk about the house that time forgot. You should see it, it looks the same way it did when I lived there, only there're piles and piles of stuff in my room. Like, towering piles. I can't smell anything as a ghost, but I'm guessing that was a good thing."

"For three days?" I asked him.

"Well, mostly," he told me as he floated down to hover over the bed. "I just...I don't know, I wanted to see if it was still home, I guess." I saw pain pass over Spike's face. "I also hoped Mama's ghost was there, but she wasn't. I wasn't surprised, really. She wasn't happy there even when she was alive."

"Maybe if you'd been able to leave here right when you passed, you might have seen her," I told him as I picked out black clothing from my closet and set it on the bed behind him. "I am thrilled for you that you've been able to get out of here, Spike— despite the massacre of my perfume."

"And look!" he said, pointing to his head. "My hair's growing! The sides of my shaved head are growing in. Isn't that wild? How can my hair grow if I'm a ghost?"

"You're changing, and getting more control of yourself. Eventually, you'll be able to just will yourself to look any way you want," I told him as I pulled out a pair of black shoes and tossed them by the bed. "Can you go anywhere now?"

"Not outside the town," Spike shook his head no. "I tried to visit the greyhound track, but I couldn't get beyond the town proper. I can make it to Holy Grove Church and no further. It's like there's a boundary around the town or something."

I frowned. That didn't sound right, and I told Spike that.

"Well, it's *there*," he repeated. "Like a glass wall. Kind of like the barrier that kept me in this building all those years," he said, and suddenly he stared down. Gideon wandered up to him wagging his tail and barked. It got a half-grin out of Spike, but his smile faded back into gloom.

"What's wrong?" I asked him.

"I suppose you'll want me to go, now," the ghost mumbled without glancing up. I blinked. It hadn't occurred to me for a while that Spike would, ultimately, leave—even when he disappeared. Now that he could, it didn't feel right to make him go. The truth was, I had gotten used to having the ghostly roommate.

"Spike, you're welcome to stay if you want, or go if you want," I told him. "This *was* your home for two decades. I will not force you out of it."

His face brightened, and he looked up at me.

"But like any other roommate," I told him, pointing a finger at him, "you have to respect my privacy. Go for a while if I want some alone time with—"

"Martin? Gabriel?" he asked impishly. "Liz?"

"A good book," I finished.

"Right. A book." His expression made it clear he did not think I was talking about a book.

"I need quiet periodically. I enjoy having you here, but occasionally, I like to be alone with my thoughts. Or, okay, someone romantic," I conceded. He smirked again and jabbed me, and to my astonishment, I felt it ever so slightly. "Now out. I need to take a shower and get ready."

"You got it," he said hopping up.

"And don't go all poltergeist downstairs while Martin's here! You can show off to Pepper once he's gone."

* * *

"Wow," Martin said as I strolled back into the shop. Pepper glanced up from her pad, raised an eyebrow, and looked back down. "I don't want to say that I wish people would die more often, but you look exquisite in that ensemble, ma'am." The heaping flattery made me blush ever so slightly.

"Pepper didn't tell him anything," Spike said as he hovered behind the two of them. "He was really digging her for information, though. About me. Well, what dude named Spike might have let her in."

I nodded toward Spike. "Are we ready?"

"The limo is out front," Martin said as he stood up. "I have a suit in the trunk, if you can just give me a minute to change."

"You drive around town with a suit in your trunk?"

"Only in the limo," he responded, grinning, as he stepped toward the door. Over his shoulder as he walked out, he added, "In the sports car, I keep it informal."

"Your boyfriend is a bit of the possessive type," Pepper murmured as she continued to comb through the binder in front of her.

"Not my boyfriend. What's that you're so engrossed in?" I asked her as I gestured toward the folder laid open within the notepad on her lap. She didn't see the gesture, but knew what I was talking about.

"The criminal file against you for homicide," Pepper murmured as she circled something in the folder and then wrote something down on her pad. "I dropped by the library and snagged it from the police archives cage."

"Archives?" I asked, stunned. "Mr. Maddox isn't even in the ground yet. How did the file get over to the library?"

"So, something you should know about the MEPD archives," Pepper said as she finally looked up. "The cage isn't *just* for historic case files. The department puts files there that it doesn't want people looking into. Too many people at the office walking in and out of the station itself, I guess. When Clutterbuck wants to hide something, the file makes its way over to the archives." Pepper said *archives* with air quotes.

"But the case is still open. They're trying to pull my certificate of occupancy."

"This is the case against you for homicide," she said as she picked up the folder and waved it. "The homicide case? *That* was over as soon as they ruled the death accidental."

"How did you even know it was there?"

"Irma Sperling is more wily than she looks," Pepper said as she lifted her eyebrows and referenced the old librarian. "She knew as soon as Clutterbuck came in with an individual file for the cage they were trying to hide something. She texted me," Pepper replied, and then puckered her lips. "Well, not texted. We have an encrypted app we use to communicate that the police couldn't subpoena so there's no record of our—"

"Conspiracy? Okay," I said as I sat down. "Then what are they hiding?"

The bells on the door clanged as Martin walked back in carrying a heavy garment bag and a shoe box. After a brief exchange directing him to the third floor, I turned back to Pepper once his footsteps faded.

"Who picked up the statue to take to the Maddoxes'?" she asked me.

"Um...Serpentine Moving?" I told her as I stood up and went behind the counter to find the paperwork. "They sent three men, came with a box truck."

"Right, okay, let's see who they are," she said as she pulled out a tablet and typed it in. Pepper frowned as she scrolled. "Would you be shocked to learn there *is* no Serpentine Moving?"

"In the county?" I asked as I yanked out the receipt.

"In the United States," she replied. "There's a Serpentine Office Removal in Australia, but nope. Nothing by that name anywhere. Did you find that paper?"

"Yeah, here it is," I passed it to her. "See? Serpentine Moving."

"With a post office box for an address?" she pointed. "A moving company has fleets of trucks. They have to have a physical address because those trucks need to be *someplace*. And you can't register a vehicle to a post office box."

"I didn't catch that," I told her. "Though, you know, it could just be where they get their mail, Pepper."

"Did you recognize the people that picked up the statue?" she asked me as she went on typing feverishly on her tablet. I told her no. "Not from your trip to the track, or maybe a familiar face you saw through the window? Someone who came into the shop?"

"No, I'd never seen them before."

"There *is* no Serpentine Moving," Pepper said finally, laying down the tablet. "No corporation registered with the state, no DBA on file with the county. Nothing. It doesn't exist."

Now I frowned. "But *Hugh* was the one that told me they were coming by to get it. No one else showed up later that day. That doesn't make any sense."

"That Hugh would send a shadow company of thugs to pick up the statue, take it somewhere and paint it silver, and then bring it to his house knowing it would kill him?" Pepper asked. "No, it makes little sense. Unless, of course, the piece didn't kill him."

Pepper reached in and threw a fragment of broken ceramic, one side painted silver, on the table in front of us. "That piece of your statue? That paint? It's not conductive."

"*Where* did you get that?"

"The archives are like a tomb of buried secrets, Fortuna," Pepper told me with a glance over her shoulder toward the library. "There's only one type of silver liquid that's conductive, and it's for painting and repairing tiny electronics. You can buy it in containers of 20 grams. To paint that statue they would have needed *hundreds* of containers, if not thousands. And even if they did, that paint? It couldn't electrocute a man to death. Not even close."

"But wouldn't there have been electrical burns?" I quizzed her.

"Only in 81 percent of cases," she told me as she drew out a printed report from the stack and passed it to me. "In 19 percent of death by electrocution cases, there were no electrical burns or current marks on the body."

"So how did they determine it was even electrocution?"

She passed me another paper from the bundle of papers in her lap. "The pacemaker recorded several electrical surges at the time of death. That's the long and the short of how they decided it electrocuted him. Well, that, and the buzz everyone heard. The thing is, though, the pacemaker had the ability to act as a defibrillator."

"So...wait, are you saying this could have been an accident? That the device in his chest malfunctioned?"

"So...I haven't gotten that far yet, actually," Pepper responded as she glowered at the papers in front of her. "Here's what I know. That paint couldn't carry enough of a current to kill him even if it was conductive—which I'm not convinced it was. The pacemaker registered a sequence of strong shocks, and if *it* sent the series of shocks, it could have killed him. That seems the most reasonable scenario, honestly."

"Okay, so it was an accident, probably—"

"Except that there's nothing *at all* in the logs they recovered that says the *device* did that *on its own*. Those events *should* have been recorded in the pacemaker's logs," Pepper pointed out. "If the pacemaker initiated them, that information is not in the logs."

"Or someone edited the logs," I reasoned.

"Right, I thought of that, but then the question becomes where or when those logs were edited," Pepper said as she sat forward. "In the device itself? By the tech that pulled the logs after he was dead? Or at the police department?"

"If the device itself, that means someone hacked his pacemaker."

"Right, and if *someone* hacked the pacemaker to edit the logs, that means someone could have hacked it in order to kill him."

I sat back and exhaled. "It's thin. I mean, it's a logical theory, but as far as proof of any of this? It's thin."

"This is Mystic's End," Pepper pointed out. "It's *always* thin. And this doesn't even venture into why *you* were connected to this little tragedy to take the blame. Why—"

"Maddox Electric," I blurted out. Pepper stopped speaking and stared at me quizzically. "Maddox Electric is the company the police department consulted with to test the statue's electric conductivity. Gabe told me."

Pepper frowned and began leafing through the folder she had, trying to find any mention of them. "There's nothing here at all about them. Nothing about the tests they did, or that they were used. Just a printout of the results as if the police tested the paint themselves. And on this paper, it claims the paint could have carried enough electricity to kill him. Even though no paint exists that could."

"If that report was faked, too, this *wasn't* an accident," I told Pepper. "Someone killed that man.

Had to have killed him. Why *else* would they hide that Hugh's brother's company tested the paint?"

"Bob Maddox is a close friend of the chief," Pepper mused as she sat back and looked off into the distance. "Question is, does Clutterbuck know? Or does he just *suspect* and hide the information just in case?"

"Just in case of what?" Martin asked as he hopped down the stairs to rejoin us. "Ladies," he nodded. Holding out his arms, he spun around to show off his charcoal gray suit. "No greyhound hair on me anywhere?" he asked.

Pepper rolled her eyes and turned back to me, ignoring Martin. "You know who has box trucks?" she asked me. "The electrical company. They've got, like, ten of 'em, I think."

"You look fine, Martin, no hair," I told him and looked at Pepper. "You think his *brother* killed him?"

"I don't know," she mused thoughtfully. "But this funeral? This funeral will be *very* interesting."

THIRTEEN

The chapel was crowded with gossiping townsfolk clustered in groups. The whispers stopped cold as if the funeral attendants had organized their reaction to my entrance. I gulped.

"Maybe I shouldn't have come," I murmured to Pepper. "I mean, they thought I killed the guy."

"Look at their expressions," Pepper whispered back. "They *still* think you killed the guy. Come on. Maybe your presence will rattle someone who knows something, and they'll slip up."

The whispers slowly returned as their eyes shifted away from me.

"Ms. Delphi," a woman's voice said sharply behind me. I spun and came face to face with Della

Maddox, the grieving widow. Standing close to her, his hand on her elbow, was the man I saw her huddled with at the party right after her husband keeled over lifeless.

"Mrs. Maddox, I'm so sorry for your loss," I told her respectfully.

"*Are* you?" she asked snidely. "I can't believe you would have the *nerve* to show your face here. You should be in *jail*."

The gossipy murmuring fell silent again.

"What for, *exactly*, Mrs. Maddox?"

"Whatever possessed you to use paint like *that* on that statue, I can't even *imagine*," she continued, her eyes narrowing and her voice rising. I recognized suddenly that Mrs. Maddox had come in from the *outside* of the church—as if she and her companion had been standing by, waiting for me to arrive.

"I didn't use silver paint on the statue, Mrs. Maddox," I replied coolly. Martin tensed next to me as the widow's expression grew even angrier. "When the men you sent over picked it up, that piece was white."

"Liar!"

"Um, Mrs. Maddox?" a timid-looking Azalea Cotton, one of my teenage students, walked back toward us from the front of the church. "Miss Fortuna is telling the truth," she told the angry woman. "I was there sketching the angel right before people came to pick it up." Her eyes darted to me and back to the widow Maddox. "It was white. Not silver. I'm sure of it."

"Did *you* see the delivery men pick it up, young woman?" Della Maddox snapped, studying the fearful girl fiercely.

"Well, no, but I did see—"

"Precisely. Not only did you *ruin* Hugh's statue for his beloved father Tiberius with that slop paint job so it's worthless," Della said as she strode forward and scowled at me, "you sent my husband to the great beyond in such a horrid way! In front of all his friends! It was *mortifying!*"

I've heard death described a lot of ways. Mortifying was a first, and I wondered whether she was talking about Hugh, or herself. I had also never spoken to a recently widowed woman worried about the valuation of the statue she thought killed her husband.

Unless...she knew it *didn't* kill her husband.

"Joe, take me to my seat," Della Maddox said to the man next to her, her voice growing breathy as she wavered on her Louboutin heels. "This woman and her lies...I'm feeling faint, Joe."

"Of course, Della," the mild-mannered man said as he put his arm around her. His eyes sought out Martin's and he nodded before accompanying the emotional widow toward the front of the church.

"Who was that with her?" I asked Martin. "Do you know him?"

"That's Joe Arturo," Martin answered as we moved away from the door. "He was Hugh's business partner in the hot dog stand at the track. I guess he's Della's partner now," he said distractedly as he watched them walk away. "Nice guy."

"Oh, yeah. He's a nice guy whose hand just patted the widow's *rear end* before she sat down," Pepper said, watching them like a hawk as they walked toward the front. "I'm sure he's a prince among men."

"What?" I asked, appalled. Turning, I peered after them, but there was nothing to see. The two of them shook hands and nodded, at least a foot apart.

"I saw it, I'm telling you," she said as she turned back and grabbed my hand. "Come on. Considering what he told Angie and feeling up the widow at her husband's funeral, I'm now even *more* convinced that he has something to do with all this."

"Ow," I said as I stumbled after her. "Where are we going?"

"To examine the body."

* * *

I didn't want to examine the body.

I thought the whole *exhibiting the dead* thing was just weird. Once people's spirits left them, they were just hollow shells of nothing. For a telepath, the lack of any kind of spirit was...uncomfortable.

"Is he here?" Pepper whispered as we stood over the casket.

"He's right there," I whispered back, pointing. "Something wrong with your eyesight?"

"That's *not* what I mean," she whispered back forcefully. "His ghost, Fortuna. His spirit. Is he attending his own funeral? Because I sure would, especially if someone tried to off me. Is *he* here?"

I looked around the large room, but everyone appeared to be mortal, and I told her so.

"Darn," she said as her eyes swept over him.

"Hey," I said as I spotted the blue orchid pinned to Hugh's black suit. It looked withered and a little the worse for wear, but I was sure it was identical to the one Hugh Maddox had worn to the party. "That boutonniere? I think he was wearing it the night he died."

"Are you sure?" Pepper asked, squinting. "That thing would have been submerged in the fountain when he went down. There'd be no reason to take it out and get it back in shape for burial unless it had some special meaning to him, or—"

"It was evidence of a felony," I hissed back.

Pepper and I stared at one another and then back at the boutonniere sitting on Hugh Maddox's chest.

"Can you fidget-finger another one, one that looks pr*ecisely* like that?" Pepper asked me as she leaned closer.

"Right now?" I asked her, confused.

"No, Fortuna, in a week or so after he's six feet under the ground, right along with the evidence that could clear you and catch *his* killer," Pepper whispered snidely. "Yes, *now!*"

I searched around to see if anyone was close, and my eyes darted trying to spot where to hide the crowd's view of my hands.

I gulped as I realized the only place my hands would be unnoticed was if I slid them down into the coffin next to Hugh Maddox.

I looked at Pepper again with a pleading look.

"Hurry!" she hissed.

I plunged my hands into the satin depths of the casket and whispered Gunther's duplication spell. In a second, I had an identical boutonniere. And then another. And then another.

I cursed and promptly cast another spell for the first spell to stop. In the end, we had one real boutonniere, and four replications.

"Hey, *maybe* we can use that," Pepper said, her

eyes alight as she reached in without a second thought and yanked the original boutonniere off Hugh using a handkerchief. She quickly pinned a carbon copy to his chest, seized the other three, and crammed them in her backpack. "Thanks. Let's go back before someone gets suspicious."

As I turned, I caught Martin across the room watching me closely.

* * *

Thirty minutes later, Reverend Kane stood on the stage to extol the virtues—and condemn the sins—of Hugh Maddox, philandering rich guy. I don't know why Pepper thought Hugh would show up to this.

If I was Hugh, and I knew Kane?

I wouldn't have shown up to this. It seemed like the whole town did, though. People stood against the wall on the side of the huge room to hear the service.

"Our poor, departed friend died far too soon," Kane said as he paced in front of the still open casket. "Had he done more with his life, had he lived by the doctrines we are required to live by— faithfulness, honesty—perhaps he would have been given more time."

"Here we go," Pepper said from my right as

Martin sat to my left. I looked through the crowd and was surprised to find that Miss Bessie and Gabriel were not in the pews. It didn't seem like Miss Bessie to miss a Mystic's End event of this magnitude. "Keep your ears peeled. Dexter Kane never heard a secret about someone he didn't spill at their funeral."

"Did our venerated friend have multiple girlfriends, disgracing his wife time and time again?" Reverend Kane asked the crowd. The crowd answered his question with silence. "Why, yes...yes, he did."

A woman wept loudly behind me.

"Did our cherished friend dismiss the concerns of his employees when they suggested working six days a week was too much? Yes, yes, he did," Reverend Kane nodded vigorously as his eyes searched out the congregants. "Did he refuse to give his wife children, disregarding the holy plan for him? Yes," Kane nodded decisively, his eyes alight. "Did we love him any less for his human imperfections?"

Reverend Kane waited, expectantly.

When no one answered, his eyes narrowed.

"No!" one person shouted. A chorus of agreement followed.

"I'm glad the only thing he had against Spike

was his mohawk," I jokingly whispered to Pepper, who nodded. "This is just crazy."

When I turned back, Martin was studying me with a question in his eyes. I grinned at him and swung back to the Reverend's rousing indictment of Hugh Maddox and tried to look absorbed by his litany, but it seemed like an eternity before I felt Martin's eyes turn away.

Oops.

"Now, was he *all* wrong? Of course not!" Reverend Kane boomed as he flung his arms wide. Then he pointed to an awkward looking young man standing along the wall. I realized it was the same young man I'd seen at the party, and later on the street with Evangeline Laroux. "When Bob's son, Lester, needed money to go to UCLA because his grades were too poor to get a scholarship, did Hugh turn him away? No! Because that's what brothers do!"

Bob's son Lester turned a brilliant crimson.

"Does he mean spiritual brothers, or *brothers* brothers?" I mumbled to Pepper.

"Bob Maddox is Hugh's brother," she mumbled back. "The one that operates Maddox Electric? Lester is his son, Hugh's nephew. He went off for some engineering degree."

"I thought the family was rich?"

"They have some kind of old-fashioned *eldest*

son inherits it all thing going on," Pepper breathed. "Once Tiberius died, Bob didn't get a thing unless Hugh gave it to him. I heard Hugh was basically running everything for his father, even before he died."

An overly made-up woman in front of us twisted and hushed us vehemently. "Don't you two have *any* respect for the dead?" she asked shrilly. Eyeing us up and down, she rolled her eyes and muttered, "Look at who I'm talking to. Of course you don't." The woman next to her nodded judgmentally and patted her hand.

"Hugh Maddox, for all his faults, was a benevolent philanthropist, giving freely to this church annually," Reverend Kane said, nodding. "I have no doubt that his lovely widow, unfettered from his sin and ignominy, will still continue to uphold in praise of him those things that her husband valued that were pure and good."

"Fat chance," someone snarled. Kane frowned as his eyes scoured the pews.

"Let us pray," he snapped and bowed his head. "The good Lord knows that Mystic's End is *certainly* in need of it."

* * *

O nce the service ended, Evangeline Laroux made her entrance.

And what an entrance it was.

Dressed all in black, she swaggered as she made her way deliberately up to the front of the pews. Once there, she started a staggered beeline for Della Maddox. Lester Maddox, still against the wall, turned pale as his eyes followed her.

Whether her gait was an attempt to be sexy, or she was cork-high and bottle-deep, I couldn't tell.

"You *owe* me," Evangeline drawled fiercely. "You're a few sandwiches short of a picnic if you think I'm gonna just take a seat in the back row with the others and pretend that—"

"Ms. Laroux, this is my *husband's* funeral—"

"Oh, yeah," she taunted. "Who's more of a wife? The one that lives with him or the one that lays—"

"*All right*, now, Ms. Laroux, this is not the time or the place," Dexter Kane said as he forcefully grabbed Angie and jerked her away from Della Maddox. "Come with me, young woman," he said furiously as he frogmarched her toward a door off the dais.

"She owes me! She knows it!" the platinum blonde screeched as she disappeared beyond the door.

"And I thought the *service* was exciting,"

Pepper mumbled as she dragged out her notebook and started jotting down Evangeline Leroux's exact words. She looked back toward the last pew and the young, pretty, seductive looking women that were hastily evacuating the church in twos and threes.

"What was that all about?"

"If I had to guess, since Boozy Barbie over there was sleeping with Hugh Maddox? She wants to make sure everyone knows she was first among mistresses," Pepper said as she nodded toward the back row. "Those women? They're the strippers and hookers of mistresses past."

"I, um...I didn't know that," I said as I turned and noticed an unreasonable number of leather miniskirts among the departing female parishioners. "I thought when Miss Bessie said there were a lot of prostitutes in this town, she was pulling my leg."

"Nope, she wasn't pulling your leg," Pepper told me as she put her backpack away. "But *they* will for a fee, if that's what you're into."

"Yeah, I didn't need to know that."

"Hey, no judgment here," Pepper said, shrugging. "Whatever floats your boat."

"Okay, Pepper, enough," I told her seriously.

We both started as the lid of the casket slammed shut.

"Well, if you were a perpetrator, you'd be feeling pretty darn safe right about now. At least if this thing contains what I think it does," Pepper said as she watched the men wheel Hugh Maddox out of the room. "You mind if I skip the burial?" she asked as she spun back to me. "I want to get back to your shop and start looking at this boutonniere."

"I'll come with you—"

"No, you and Martin go to the interment," she said, shaking her head. "I want a firsthand account of what transpires there. And if someone throws themselves into the hole *with* Hugh," she said, handing me a small camera, "get pictures. I'll meet you at the after party."

"It's called a reception," I corrected her, frowning. Pepper had calmed down a bit since I'd known her, but her blunt manner of speaking still caught me off guard sometimes. "There's no after-party. Reception."

"Okay, *reception*," she said with exaggerated piety. "Meet you there?"

"Let me give you a key in case Spike isn't there—"

"I've got one."

"I didn't give you one," I told her.

"Nope, but I've got one. Bye!" she said as she made for the exit. I sighed and turned around—

—to find Martin staring at me.

"I don't mean to sound like a broken record," he said as he leaned in, "but who, exactly, is Spike?"

FOURTEEN

"You said we should keep our secrets," I told Martin as he prodded me on the way to the Maddox Estate. Hugh Maddox was to be buried on the land where he had lived—and died—in a private family cemetery.

"I did," Martin responded as he stroked his stubbled chin. "Perhaps I've changed my mind."

"Well, perhaps it's not up to you," I told him. "Or, well, not only you."

"Feisty woman," he murmured, grinning.

"If you think *that* was feisty, Martin, you will be incredibly surprised when you *really* see feisty," I told him even though I smiled back. He wasn't being pushy or demanding, and he *was* asking in a pretty charming manner. "Keep pushing on this, and I *might* show it to you."

"Just tell me this...do I have anything to worry about?"

"In what way?" I asked.

"Well, I'm competing for your affections with Gabriel Wilcox, though I think I have that competition thwarted. Granted, he helped me along by serving a search warrant on you *and* accusing you of murder," Martin said with a twinkle in his eye. "But even so, I'm not too worried about dear old Gabe. Not exactly."

"You're not, huh?"

"No. I think I'm more worried about Miss Bessie. She's a fierce competitor on his behalf. No man could have a greater champion if he went out to search for one."

I laughed.

"If there *is* a third contender for your heart, I would like to suss out whether this third player is a competitor that I *should* worry about," Martin told me.

"First, I'd like to point out I'm not a prize to be won," I told him, holding up one finger. "Second, you have no claims on me—so even if I *was* seeing someone, I'm not really obligated to tell you about it, am I?"

"Of course not," Martin grinned widely. "Why

do you think I'm trying to be so charming about my questions?"

I laughed again.

"Any obligations people feel are their own choices to feel, Fortuna. Obligations cannot be extracted or demanded, no matter what other men may think," he said, his grin fading a bit. "I am not owed an explanation, but I *would* like to know, if you'll tell me."

"Third," I continued, tilting my head. "Spike is a friend. More like a brother, really. There is no possibility, none, that he and I would ever be romantically involved. That much I will tell you."

"Have you known him long?" Martin asked casually.

"I met him when I came to Mystic's End. He's a good guy, we're friends, and there's nothing more to it," I lied casually. Well, it wasn't a lie, really—what I said was accurate. Just not fully truthful. Refusing to volunteer information wasn't really lying—right?

"Well, then I hope to meet him soon," Martin said with utter conviction as he bowed his head.

I didn't respond. There was no way I could without telling Martin more, and I wasn't ready to do that yet. I didn't know if I ever would be.

He was, though, wearing me down.

It was easier to keep things from him when he showed up with dinner twice a week and then left after a few hours. This week for the most part, the man hadn't left my side since the search warrant thing, and it was harder to not slip and say something I shouldn't.

Just his presence, his smile...it was wearing away the sharp edges. Making me wonder why, dinner after dinner, I held him at arm's length and refused to take that single step that would start something more.

Well, okay, he could have been my brother or something...

But now?

A date. *Just* one date. Why was I refusing?

He's handsome, kind, has a very successful job —though that didn't mean much to me. We grew up in the same type of environment and, from some things he'd said, it seemed we both rejected some of the excesses of that upbringing. We both had secrets that caused us pain, and we both respected (mostly) the other's choice to keep those secrets hidden.

Maybe *that* was it, I sighed.

The fear of him disappearing if I *really* told him who I was. Not wanting to take a risk because I enjoyed being around him, but not wanting to go forward because—

"What?" Martin asked, his forehead furrowing with concern. "Why the sigh?"

"You ever wonder whether you're making the right choice?" I asked him sincerely. "You always seem so confident, so sure of yourself. Don't you...doubt?"

His eyes opened wide as if my question had truly astounded him. He thought for a moment as his eyes locked on mine, and then said slowly, "Of course. I'm human. Doesn't everyone? Doubt is part of the human condition, Fortuna. I'm not superhuman."

Well, *I* am.

And I'm still a mess of confusion and doubt sometimes.

* * *

Joe Arturo stuck to Della Maddox's side like glue at the gravesite. Slightly behind her, Bob Maddox and his son Lester stood looking glum as Reverend Dexter Kane started up *again* on Hugh's sins of the flesh.

"Do we really have to hear this twice?" I whispered to Martin.

"Why do you think I only showed up *here*?" Miss Bessie whispered fiercely as she waddled up to me, Gabe helping to support her. "Well, that, and there was no food at the church. I go where the canapés are, I do."

"Quiet!" a woman hissed. "How rude!"

"What are *you* on about, Marla Dinkins?" Miss Bessie snapped at the woman looking at her judgmentally. "Don't think I didn't notice you shoving the cheddar beignets in your fat face at Todd's funeral like they were going out of style!"

The woman glared at Miss Bessie and then grabbed the man with her. They moved with due haste to the other side of the crowd.

"Gram, settle down," Gabe whispered. "Fortuna," he nodded. Glaring at my escort, I *think* he then muttered *Martin* in Martin's general direction but I couldn't be sure. It could have just as easily been tartan.

But it probably wasn't.

Miss Bessie shook off Gabe's arm and fiercely pushed in between Martin and me, shoving him about a foot away. Martin hid a smile behind a cough and whispered "I told you. Fierce competitor."

"Shut up, Salvi, can't you see a man's getting buried here!" Miss Bessie shouted so loud that Reverend Dexter Kane stopped his preaching, his face angry. He had been on quite a roll about a mistress and strippers and artwork and sins. Miss Bessie's outburst had killed his momentum.

Martin Salvi looked completely and utterly charmed by the snide old woman while Gabe looked like he wanted to crawl under the nearest rock. His face was red, his expression mortified.

"So, tell me," Bessie whispered loudly as she stretched her short body towards my ear. "What have you and Pepper found out about Hugh? I know that you're working on it."

"Well, we kind of have to," I whispered back. "They think I killed the guy with my magic silver paint."

The old woman gasped.

"You *didn't* use magic paint, did you?" Miss Bessie looked horrified.

"It *wasn't* magic, I *didn't* paint the statue, and I *didn't* kill him—accidentally or otherwise," I whispered back to her. "I think you're a little out of the loop. This isn't the time or the place to catch you up, though."

Miss Bessie stared at me, shocked.

"What a *terrible* thing to say to an old woman, child," she snapped.

"Well, there are people all around, Miss Bessie," I told her, my eyes scanning the crowd. Several people around us appeared to be listening to Kane's treatise on adultery, but a few heads were ever so slightly turned toward Bessie and me.

"I mean that I'm out of the loop. Horrible. *Horrible.* And we can't have that, so let's go," Bessie said, tugging on my arm.

"The funeral isn't over—"

"Fortuna Delphi, are you going to deny an old, feeble woman the right to go to the bathroom?" Miss Bessie screeched as she peered up at me. Kane stopped again and stared at us. "My bladder isn't what it used to be and Kane won't be done until I'm a puddle on the floor! And if I turn into a puddle on the floor, you know what will have started that puddle? A big, yellow—"

"Ms. Delphi, take the old woman to the house!" Della shouted, staring at me angrily. "One of the servants can drive you both there in the golf cart."

"Thank you—"

"And just *stay* there," she said menacingly. "The clergyman will be done with his service in just a few minutes. *Won't* you, Dexter? We will all be along shortly."

* * *

Once we entered the house, Miss Bessie shook my arm off and headed, steady, to the main staircase as if she were a competitive speed walker.

"You can walk?" I asked her as I followed her up.

"I can walk," she responded as we raced up the stairs. "Come on, Hugh's office is the last door on the left."

"If you can walk *this* fast," I demanded as I struggled to keep up, "why on earth do you—"

"Pretend to be a feeble old woman that can't take two steps without help?" she asked me over her shoulder, gray hair flying out of the confines of her bun. "I could live on my own just fine, but Gabe likes to feel he's doing something for me. It's much easier to stay up on all the gossip living there. You should see the hot orderly that gives the sponge baths."

"They do not have a man doing that!"

"Magic *has* its benefits, girl," she told me. "They may not realize they have a man doing it, but oh, yes, Beau—"

"I don't want to hear it. That's horrible! It's practically sexual assault, Miss Bessie."

"Oh ho, I wish," she quipped.

"As for Gabe, you know, you could just ask him to take you out to dinner," I huffed. She was far, far quicker than I would have ever thought she was. "That would be easier than living a full-time charade."

"I like Claire, and I enjoy going places with her. That, and if they think you can't walk? They wait on you hand and foot *like a queen* at the home. In here, quick," she said as she opened a large wooden door and slammed it shut behind us.

"What are we doing here?" I asked.

"There's *something* in here you need," she told me. Looking around, Miss Bessie brightened. "And *I* need that potted plant," she said as she marched toward a huge ficus in the corner, wiggled her fingers and created a sparkling toilet seat floating over the soil.

Before I could protest, she had dropped her pantyhose and jumped on the levitating thing.

"Oh my goodness," I said as I turned around and looked out the window to give her some privacy.

With a sigh, I heard liquid running.

"Ugh," I muttered.

"What? I said *you* needed something in here, I didn't say I didn't *really* have to pee like a racehorse, did I?" The sound of liquid running ended, and I felt a whoosh of magic. "You can turn around now, Miss Prude."

"How do you know I need something in here?" I asked, turning around. The air was thick with the smell of roses.

"I don't know. I just know things, and I *realize* you do. Couldn't tell you more than that since I slapped you and passed down all the really good magic," she said as she sat down on one of the two chairs in front of the desk, "I don't get as much as I used to."

"Can you give me a clue?"

"I did, I *mentioned* it's in this office. You want a map, lazy?" Miss Bessie snapped. "Use your powers, girl, and get to searching."

"You pretend to be almost ready for a wheelchair so people will wait on you, and *I'm* lazy?" I said as I started shuffling through the papers on the desk.

"What are you doing?" she demanded incredulously.

I stopped and looked up at her. "Looking?"

"With your *eyes?*" she asked, even more incredulous.

"Well...yeah...I mean—"

"Whoever trained you should be slapped upside their head," Miss Bessie said as she stood up and mumbled about my not knowing even the most rudimentary magic. "Watch closely."

Miss Bessie made three defined gestures with her fingers and whispered *ostende mihi*. I felt the surge of energy and waited, but nothing happened.

"I don't get it," I told her.

"That's the spell to have the universe show you what it *wants* you to know," Miss Bessie told me impatiently. "Most of the time, the universe doesn't care what you know or don't know, but in *this* case, it does. I think it's annoyed that a symbol of hope was used to take someone out."

"But nothing happened."

Miss Bessie rolled her eyes so hard that I thought her eyeballs would fall out of her head.

"That's because the universe showed *me* I needed to bring you *here*," she told me as she poked a finger in my arm. "Universe already presented *me* with what I need to do. It will not show *me* what *you* need to do. *You* need to ask for that guidance."

I took a deep breath and nodded. Then I mimicked her hand gestures and whispered the words she had. This time, the whoosh produced a wind that knocked two papers off the desk.

"That's it?" I asked as the energy faded away.

"What do you want, the Goddess *herself* to come down and hand you a typewritten report?" Miss Bessie asked and then muttered curses and complaints to herself while pointing at the sheets on the floor. "Go look at them!"

I hurried over and grabbed the papers. Scanning, my eyes widened.

"Well?"

"It's a life insurance policy," I told her after I read through them. "Della had life insurance on Hugh, the policy bought...let me see...just two months ago."

"They're richer than Midas, why would she do that?" Miss Bessie asked.

"She's not the beneficiary."

"Who is?"

"Joe Arturo...and Bob Maddox."

"The business partner and the brother?"

I nodded. "They each get five million dollars... no, wait...ten million dollars. It has an Accidental Death rider," I said as I looked up from the papers. "The payout doubled because the death was accidental."

"Only you don't think it was," Miss Bessie said.

"No," I shook my head. "I don't think it was. I think someone killed him and tried to blame my angel for it." I looked down at the pages and whispered the duplication spell. The pages copied...and then copied again...and again...

Miss Bessie slapped her head. "*Unus*! It means one! Tell it *one* copy!" She stared at me as I hastily uttered the stop spell and the papers stopped creating more of themselves. "You use *two* spells when *one* would work just as well? Ugh, Fortuna," Miss Bessie shook her head. "*Who* taught you this?"

"I had some training with a coven in Mickwac—"

"There's no coven there besides a mortal coven."

"Yes, Avalon Grove," I nodded as Miss Bessie's face transformed into an expression of utter horror. "They helped—"

"Do you mean to tell me you, a *witch*, were trained *in magic* by a group of human, mortal *wanna-be-witches?"* she asked with a slow, steady, deliberate anger that was slightly terrifying.

"Look, you don't know my story—"

"I think it *may* be about time I hear it," Miss Bessie said as she crossed her arms. "Now," she pointed to the papers I had duplicated, snapped as she whispered *ire*, and looked at me once the copies I created disappeared. "Do it again, and this time, make *one* copy."

I sighed and tried again.

I had never been so happy a new spell worked on the first try.

FIFTEEN

When I finished talking, Miss Bessie stared at me, her face unreadable.

It wasn't a long story.

I told her about walking into a magical circus; how my powers were awakened by the circus because there was a paranormal somewhere in my ancestry. How the Witches' Council, a powerful group that governed all paranormals, decree that all humans or half-humans in the paranormal towns and circuses be killed. I described how my friend, Charlotte, used her ringmaster power to turn me into a full paranormal of my choice to protect me from execution.

"So they gave you a *decision to make,* let you be

anything you wanted—and you *chose* to be a witch?" Miss Bessie asked as we sat in a small alcove off the dining room. The table was laden with after-par—um, reception food, and my stomach growled. "You could have been a vampire, a werewolf, a fairy, even a *dragon*—and you decided to be a witch?"

I nodded.

"I would have picked a dragon. Anyway. And who is your familiar?" she asked.

I blinked. "I don't have one. I mean, Charlotte and Gunther had familiars, but I thought they only had them *because* they were ringmasters."

Miss Bessie looked at me thoughtfully.

Then she sighed.

"Maybe I slapped too soon, thinking you were ready," the old woman told me, her eyes narrowing.

"Ready for what?"

"I *assumed*, since you were the first female full-witch I'd seen in this town since *I* was born. I figured you were the one I was waiting for," Miss Bessie said as she looked out the window of the alcove and watched the mourners gathered around Hugh's coffin. "The one who would take my burden from me. Now, don't get me wrong. You *are*," she told me quickly. "You are."

"What burden?"

"I'm an old lady, Fortuna," the old woman smiled at me, her watery eyes blinking. "My magic has...*shifted* as I age. I am in my gray season, and that comes with certain...limitations. Limitations that I hoped you wouldn't have...but it seems you have your own just the same," she sighed and passed her hand over her face.

"I don't understand what you're saying," I told her, shaking my head.

"And you *won't*," Miss Bessie warned. "Not until you're ready to hear it all."

For the second time that day, I wondered to myself what I was afraid of. Why I stood on the edge and refused, just *refused*, to jump.

"I can see it in your face," Miss Bessie told me. Her expression was faintly disapproving, and a trifle hurt. "You're not ready. Not ready to know, not ready to be."

"Be what?"

"Do you *want* me to answer that?"

I paused. After a few moments, I asked her if I had to know.

"No, of course not," Miss Bessie shook her head. "You can go through life never digging deeper, unburdened by the decisions of the past that affect you." The old woman spoke to me warmly, even fondly, while the subtle disapproval remained etched across her face. "You can live here and use your magic to paint pictures and play detective with your friend Pepper. You *can* choose that, yes," Miss Bessie nodded.

"Or?"

"Or, child, you can be what you were destined to be. You can know who and what you are," Miss Bessie said, the disapproval vanishing, her eyes sparkling.

"Whenever someone talks about witches and destiny, my stomach gets a little queasy," I told her.

"Eh, you already *are* what you were meant to be," Miss Bessie said as she waved a dismissive hand. "If you want me to be honest, *your* destiny? Already fulfilled. I passed the power. *You* have it. The story could end there. I've done my part."

"You don't *seem* like you think you have," I observed.

Miss Bessie glanced out the window and spied the crowd walking up the hill toward the house. "No, no, I don't suppose I believe I have done all I can do," the old woman said with a sigh. "But what I have to tell you *will* change how you feel about this town, Fortuna, and the people in it. Maybe even yourself. Your birth parents. But you should get the choice to make that change. I was given a choice whether to take up the mantle of mystic, too."

"You were?"

"I was," she said as she looked back at me. "I can promise you I never regretted making the choice that I did."

* * *

Pepper arrived just as the wealthy crowd began tearing apart the table of food like it was after church on a Sunday at the local discount buffet.

"I got *some* news, but not here," she whispered as she hugged me. The embrace shocked me until I realized Pepper was using my hair to cover the fact that she was talking to me.

"Hey, did you ever get the insurance papers?" I whispered back.

"No, they weren't in the database. I checked."

"*I* did," I whispered.

"You did what?"

"I got the insurance papers. Snatched 'em right off of Hugh's desk upstairs. They're in my purse."

"I am impressed at your newfound theft skills, Ms. Delphi," Pepper whispered in my ear as we continued to lock one another in an embrace. "But if you and I don't end this hug, Martin will be wondering if *we're* having an affair."

We pulled back, and Pepper winked at me.

All around us people ate and drank,

punctuating the air between bites with flowery toasts to Hugh Maddox and his life well lived. The energy of the dining hall would have been more appropriate to a wedding than a funeral.

I spotted Martin across the room and waved at him. He held up a champagne glass and nodded, but continued his discussion with someone I couldn't see.

"*Who* has champagne at a funeral?" I asked Miss Bessie and Pepper as I heard another cork pop.

"It's not a funeral, it's an after-party," Miss Bessie quipped.

"*Thank* you," Pepper said, holding her hand out. "See? I told you, didn't I? None of these people cared about Hugh Maddox." Strains of a concerto began playing in the background. "It wouldn't surprise me if a band showed up in an hour."

Miss Bessie nodded and shuffled toward the buffet.

"Well, I need to make the rounds," Pepper said as she tossed her head and scanned the crowd. "I suggest you do the same. If we split the duties, maybe it won't look as suspicious—ugh, here comes trouble."

I turned my head to see Evangeline Laroux enter the room. Her manner was more subdued than before, and her eyes cast downward. Lester Maddox left his father's side and walked over to the sultry blond. "What's that about, I wonder?" I asked.

"That's a nerdy boy with a crush on an unobtainable girl," Miss Bessie told me with her mouth full, holding a plate full of tiny hot dogs wrapped in a delicate pastry, a generous dollop of ketchup in one corner. "Lester's had a thing for her for years. Well, almost *everyone* has had a thing for her at one time or another, poor girl."

"*Poor girl?*" I asked, surprised. "That woman is a wrecking ball!"

"*You* try living your life thinking men only like you because of your big bosoms and fake hair," Miss Bessie said after she swallowed. "That poor girl couldn't have a normal relationship anymore if she *tried, at least not the way she acts.* She just...hasn't figured that out yet."

"Well, that's kind of her *own* fault, isn't it?" I asked, watching Evangeline's eyes light up as she leaned in to show off her cleavage. "She doesn't have to act like that."

"No one *has* to act like that, Fortuna," Pepper scoffed.

"But there's *usually* a reason they do," Miss Bessie said as she stared at Angie. Pressing a hand to her throat, she added, "And it's usually not a happy story."

I watched the pair for a few more moments and then announced I would go over and talk to them. Miss Bessie stared at me, her jaw dropping open filled with half-chewed mini-dogs.

"What?" I asked as I reached out to close her mouth.

"I told you that so you could have a bit more *sympathy* for the girl, not so you'd go over there and make her your new best friend," Miss Bessie said as she spotted Gabe walking over toward us.

"I'm not," I said. "I just want to say hello, tell her I don't have any hard feelings toward her."

Mostly.

"Have sympathy for the girl, but *you* keep your guard *up*. She may be a victim in my eyes, but sometimes victims can be the most dangerous people you'll ever meet—once they've had enough of the world kicking them around."

* * *

"Ms. Laroux?" I said as I walked up to her and Lester.

"What do *you* want?" she asked me as her eyes narrowed dangerously. She was so surprised to see me she forgot to affect her exaggerated drawl.

"I just wanted to talk for a minute," I nodded and held out my hand to Lester. "First, though, Mr. Maddox, I'm so sorry for the loss of your uncle. I'm sure this is a difficult time for your family. I'm Fortuna Delphi. I own the—"

"I know who you are," he answered in a nasally voice as he extended his hand. His tone was amicable, and absent the venom that had infused Della's when she spoke to me. "Aunt Della thinks you killed Uncle Hugh so, believe me, I've heard a great deal about you."

I looked at him surprised. "You don't?"

He sniffed, and it sounded like he was suffering from some terrible cold. He pulled a handkerchief from his ill-fitting jacket pocket and blew his nose loudly. "If you *did*, you made my Aunt Della's year."

"Lester, don't be *nice* to her," Evangeline snapped. "She's made my life miserable ever since she got here."

"Angie, you make *yourself* miserable," Lester told her with a knowing look. Despite Lester's nerdy appearance with choppy hair and an ill-fitting suit, he spoke with confidence and didn't seem at all cowed by Evangeline's beauty or her words. "And don't think I don't know that you used what I told you about Uncle Hugh to get Fortuna here arrested. Well, almost arrested.

We haven't talked about it, but I'm not an idiot."

"Lester, you shut your mouth!" Angie hissed at him, her eyes wide.

"It doesn't matter anymore," he rolled his eyes. "They dropped the case, so what does it matter now?" Lester turned to me. "The only reason I bring it up is I wanted to tell you I'm sorry. If I had any idea that Angie would do what she did, I never would have said anything to her that night."

"Lester!" she hissed again.

"Give it a rest, Angie. Nothing will happen to you. Your father will make sure of that," he told her quietly.

"Okay, let's back up here. *You're* the reason the police searched my shop?"

Lester looked around and then gestured for me to follow him. As he took off down a hallway, Evangeline Laroux glared at me with hatred, turned on her heel, and followed Lester. I hurried after them, glancing behind me as we turned down another dark hallway.

"So, look," Lester said after he led us unto an empty room. There were no furnishings, but the wallpaper indicated this would likely have been a nursery once. "I talked to Angie the night my uncle died."

"I don't remember you being at the party," I told her. She made a face at me and turned her back.

"She wasn't. Uncle Hugh never would have invited any of his...paramours to a party at the estate. It's simply *not done*," Lester said with an exaggerated eye roll. "After my uncle's accident, I called Angie to come over. I just...I just needed someone to talk to," he admitted. "Dad was inconsolable."

"More upset about his brother than that horrible woman was about her own husband," Angie muttered.

"I don't have many friends in this town," Lester shrugged. "A science nerd isn't the pinnacle of popularity, you know?"

"You don't live here?"

"No, I live in California," he said. "I was only in town for the garden party. I know it's billed as 'Hugh and Della's' party, but it's a *family* tradition. Not their thing alone. My dad insists that I come back for it. It was really important to my grandmother."

"How's your dad doing?" I asked him.

"He's...better," Lester said as he pinched the bridge of his nose. "I will stay a week or so more, just to make sure. But I think he'll be back at work next week. I hope."

I frowned. "Your dad hasn't been to work since the accident?"

Lester shook his head.

"Who's running Maddox Electric right now?" I asked. If Lester's father wasn't at work, the likelihood that *he* was a part of the faked electric test on the statue was low. He might not even know that his company took part in framing me.

"Joe Arturo," Lester told me. "Joe's been *amazing* through this whole thing, taking care of everything. Even my aunt. Such a great guy."

I bet.

"Anyway, getting back to why we came in here," Lester frowned. "When Angie came over, she heard my dad and me talking about the paint theory. It was really wild, but the police seemed willing to *entertain* it," Lester shrugged and leaned back against the wall. "I didn't know that Angie would take what she overheard and try to...well, I don't even know what."

"Get me arrested? Sent to prison? Convicted of negligent homicide?" I offered as I glared at Angie's back. If Lester felt enough guilt that he would repeatedly apologize to me, a stranger, Angie looked...well, the opposite of that.

"Yeah, I...I just feel like I should apologize to you. I didn't know that Angie had such an issue with you. It never would have happened if I hadn't invited her over."

Except that Gideon hadn't seen Angie Laroux slink through my house to plant silver paint in it. The outline the dog saw was clearly a man.

"So who did you get to plant silver paint at my house?" I asked her point blank.

She whirled around and stared at me in confusion.

"What are you *talking* about, Delphi?"

"The paint the police found," I lied. Her expression didn't change, and I could feel that her confusion was genuine.

She didn't know.

"Angie, did you—"

"No, Lester! I just made a phone call when I went to the little girls' room!" Angie protested. "I didn't plant *paint* anywhere! Where would I even get paint? I didn't really want her arrested, I just wanted her...harassed...a little..."

"Angie..." Lester sighed.

"Is your cell phone a business cell phone?" I asked her.

"Why do *you* care?" she shot back as she tossed her hair, and Lester glared at her. Angie bounced on her toes to a rhythm only she could hear, and then leaned against the wall to tap her foot. I waited. Lester glared. Finally, she frowned and spat "Oh, fine! Yes."

That's why the call seemed to come from the complex. They didn't bother investigating where the person was when they made the call. They just recorded the number and the address where it was registered.

Pepper was right. These people didn't investigate much at all.

They worked pretty hard at frame-up jobs, though.

"Anyway, I just wanted to apologize," Lester repeated. "I hope you can forgive Angie. She...she gets carried away with her crushes sometimes."

"A crush?" she shrieked. "What I feel for Martin *isn't a crush*, you buffoon!" Her eyes snapped angrily at Lester, but he seemed unconcerned with her outburst.

"Like I said," he told me, gesturing toward Angie.

"So, now that we're all friends again, Angie—can you *stop* with the certificate of occupancy thing?" I asked her. She looked confused again, and I sighed. It would have been too easy, I guess.

"What's that?" Lester asked.

"Mystic's End is trying to throw me out of my building because of a...a paperwork issue," I told him. "I assumed it was just part of Angie's campaign against me."

"Ooh, *that* would have been a good one," Angie's eyes lit up. Lester buried his face in his hands. "What? It doesn't involve prison time! No one gets hurt, I mean—"

"So you *didn't* do it?" I asked her.

She refused to answer me.

"Talk to Joe Arturo," Lester said when Angie didn't speak up. "His wife works in the Mystic's End Building Department. Maybe he can help you straighten it out."

SIXTEEN

As I made my way back into the soirée, I bit my lip and worried about all I'd learned. Mentally sifting through the information, I recognized there were truly only two suspects in the death of Hugh Maddox at this moment.

Joe Arturo, and Della Maddox.

Yes, I was a *little* disheartened that Evangeline Laroux didn't murder him. It would have been nice to have a legitimate reason to get that constant thorn in my side *yanked* out for a few years.

It's not like she'd have to go very far.

I mean, the penitentiary was *just* on the edge of town.

Okay, that wasn't nice.

"Did you find out anything?" Pepper asked me

as she dragged me back into the alcove. Glaring at the throng as it pushed out onto the patio, she continued, "I swear, these people are proof that evolution can *absolutely* go in reverse."

"I did, actually," I responded, and quickly related how I was reported to the tip-line, that it was clear Angie knew nothing of the paint found at the gallery, and that Bob Maddox was so torn up about his brother's death that he hadn't been to work since the accident—making it improbable he fabricated the conduction analysis.

"That doesn't mean he *didn't* do it originally, though, right?" Pepper said. "The murder, I mean? Maybe he's just wracked with guilt. Or Lester's lying. Joe Arturo stepped in *after* Hugh died, right? They sent the truck to pick up the statue *before* he did, when Bob presumably was still running Maddox Electric."

"You're assuming the truck was theirs, though," I pointed out. "We don't know that for sure. Do we?"

"No," Pepper sighed and leaned against the huge house, her face pinched up in concentration. Suddenly shoving off the wall, she glanced around again to make sure we were alone, and confided, "We *know* that there was an electronic sensor in that orchid, though. The name on the sensor was *Spritetronic*. I looked it up—they make pacemakers.

Someone *had* to have wirelessly hacked his pacemaker. I'm sure of it."

"Can you prove it?" I asked her. She shook her head no. "Were there any fingerprints on the thing you found?"

I didn't know *for sure* that Pepper could pull fingerprints, much less run them, but I had a feeling anything the police could do she could do better.

Well, not *lawfully*.

But better.

"Not that I could use," she conceded. "I think we need to circulate around the party again." Pepper looked like mingling with these people was about as inviting an idea as having a root canal with no anesthetic. "And I would like to talk to Bob Maddox. Well, not *me*. He loathes me. I mean you. If I were you, I would do that."

"Oh?" I refrained from expressing the fact that he probably assumes I killed his brother, and *perhaps* I wasn't the right person to do that, but Pepper's expression made it clear they had a past. Knowing Pepper and what may have happened in her past, maybe he *would* prefer to talk to me.

"I also picked up the will from the courthouse," Pepper told me as she leaned in, dropping her voice again. "If Della Maddox is found to have had *anything* to do with Hugh Maddox's death? *Everything* goes to Bob Maddox. Every last dime, this house, the businesses—*everything*. Even though we don't have much pointing to him, that's a heck of a motivation to kill him and try to frame her."

* * *

"What were you doing with Lester and Angie?" Martin asked me as I worked my way through the crowd of judgmental people that would tell me very little about anything because they thought I was, you know, a murderer.

"Do *you* know him?" I asked as he scowled at a stocky man that had thrust me aside roughly.

"We're acquainted, yes," Martin nodded as he accompanied me to the perimeter of the patio and handed me a cold glass of ice water. I took it gratefully. "Maddox Electric has a suite at the track, and he would come with his father when he was in town."

"I'm curious—what's the deal with him and Angie?" I asked, grateful to be gossiping for no other reason than curiosity. "Miss Bessie claimed he held a torch for her, but he didn't seem *particularly* enthralled by her when we talked."

Martin smiled. "They're friends, only that. Couldn't ever be more than that. I assume that's why Angie is so comfortable with him, actually," Martin nodded and smirked. "Lester Maddox is *very* happily wed. He and his husband look like mad scientist bookends when they stand next to each other. I think his father is still trying to accept the whole thing, so not many people know."

"Wait, Lester's *gay*?" I asked, astonished.

"Yes, why?"

"He can't be gay!"

Martin shifted uneasily. "You're not homophobic, are you?" he asked, frowning.

I stared at him. "Are you *serious*? My friend Liz is a lesbian! So's Claire, Miss Bessie's..." I trailed off, recognizing that I was dangerously close to sounding like my adoptive father when he declared he wasn't racist because he had a single black butler.

"Well, I only ask because—"

"Look, I've just never known Miss Bessie to be *wrong* about anything like that," I explained to him, and his face softened. I have to admit, the fact that he would show disapproval about homophobia *even* with a woman he was trying to date impressed me. "No, I'm not homophobic at all, Martin. I promise. It just startled me, that's all."

He nodded. "They both work for tech companies out in California. His husband's name is Ed Thornton. He does commercial lighting. In fact, his company did some lighting at the track," Martin said and then took a sip of a pink drink. I raised my eyebrow. "What?"

"*What* is *that?*" I asked him, staring in horror at his drink.

"A Shirley Temple," he answered.

"Isn't that a kid's drink?"

"Are you *sure* you're not homophobic?"

"Are *you* saying that drink is gay because it's pink and you're a man drinking it?" I challenged him wryly, my eyebrow raised. "*Now* who's cleaving to traditional gender norms?"

"First, it's *red*, and second, I am *completely* comfortable with my masculinity," Martin informed me, and then took an exaggerated sip from his Shirley Temple. "I am not watering down my manhood just by consuming an appletini, *thank* you very much." A half-smile danced on his lips.

"Ugh, you drink appletinis?"

"Have you ever tried—"

"Just *what* do you think you're doing?" Gabe asked as he stormed up to the two of us and whirled on me indignantly.

"Drinking water?" I held up the glass. "Discussing the gender norms of various alcoholic drink colors?" My quippy answer did *not* relax Gabe's face in the slightest. "What's wrong?"

"Did you take *my grandmother* with you to *steal* papers from Hugh Maddox's office?" he asked me. Perspiration glistened on his brow, but I didn't think it was from the radiant afternoon sunlight.

"Why don't you step *back*, Detective," Martin warned ominously. All the warmth and laughter in his voice had utterly vaporized. Gabe's eyes flashed over to Martin and for a moment, the Detective looked him up and down. Without answering, he spun back to me.

He did not step back.

"I didn't *steal* anything," I told Gabriel in a low voice, which wasn't a lie. Everything was there, the same as it was before I went in. "What did Miss Bessie tell you?"

I found it hard to believe that she told him *anything* at all. When Gabe found out I could see ghosts, he *didn't* seem to put two and two together that I wasn't the first woman he'd known that could do that.

"I heard Pepper and Miss—my grandmother talking. They didn't know I was listening," he stated, having the good sense to bristle a little at his admittance of snooping. In two heartbeats, his discomfort passed and his resentment flared anew. "How the hell did you get my—"

"Watch your mouth, and step back," Martin growled, taking a step forward and physically holding his arm out in front of me. "If I have to tell you a third time, Wilcox, you will *not* like where this goes."

"I'm not speaking to *you*!" Gabe shouted.

"But I *am* speaking to you."

The two men glared at each other, Martin's icy cold menace and Gabriel's fiery fury clashing invisibly between them. Just as I was about to speak, Miss Bessie slapped Gabriel from behind.

"What is wrong with you?" Miss Bessie said as she tugged on Gabe, hard. "The whole patio is watching the two of you, and this is a reception for a deceased man! I *swear*, boy, occasionally I worry you're a few bristles short of a broom when it comes to women. *What* is going on here?"

"Nothing," Gabriel said sullenly as he glowered at Martin and stepped back. "Nothing, Gram. It's nothing. Let's get out of here."

"Don't you *nothing* me, boy," Miss Bessie warned and smacked him lightly with her palm again. "I'm not going anywhere until you tell me *what* made you decide to make an idiot of yourself in the presence of all these people."

Gabriel looked at Miss Bessie, again at me, and suddenly spun around and stalked off.

"Talk," she grumbled at me as she watched Gabe pick his way through the swarm of people and escape into the house. "There's only one person who's ever gotten Gabriel *that* roiled up, and that's

Pepper." She shifted back around and faced me.
"*What* did she do now?"

"Nothing, at least as far as I know," I told her.
She studied me expectantly, but I mentioned
nothing more. It wasn't like Gabriel to be as agitated
as he was, and I didn't want to cause problems
between him and Miss Bessie by tattling on him for
eavesdropping.

Martin looked at me with a raised eyebrow, but
said nothing.

"Nothing else?" she barked at me.

"No, ma'am," I told her.

"All right, *she's* not going to say anything. What
about *you*, handsome?" Miss Bessie turned around
and eyed Martin up and down. "You wanna score
marks with me? Spill it. She may defend him, but I
imagine you'd be right as rain to get my grandson in
trouble in any way you could," she told him,
squinting. "Well?"

Martin's eyes locked on the stout old woman for
a moment, and then he raised them to examine the
crowd. "Bob!" he called as he picked up his drink
and raised it in Bob Maddox's direction. "Pardon
me, ladies," he announced to both of us, giving me a
wink.

He practically ran to give his condolences to
Hugh's brother as Miss Bessie stared after him, her
mouth agape.

Then she giggled.

"He's a shrewd one, *that* guy," Miss Bessie said with something akin to admiration as she watched Martin. "I can see why you like him."

"I do," I nodded and took a sip of water.

"My grandson heard Pepper and me talking, didn't he?" Miss Bessie asked as she turned back to me. "My ears burned too late, but I felt that someone was listening."

I sighed, not surprised she knew. No sense in covering for Gabe, I guess.

"Yes, Miss Bessie. He wasn't happy that I lugged his feeble, helpless, virtually crippled grandmother to the second floor of the house to break and enter," I told her cheerfully. "Which, since he *doesn't* know you're in better shape than *I* am, *would* be something to be ticked off about. If it were true."

"Of course he did," Miss Bessie sighed. "Though I suspect it was what he heard *and* who I was talking to that got the bee buzzing in his bonnet." Miss Bessie said a few choice curse words under her breath. "That was my fault. I should have been more careful."

"How is *him* flying off the handle *your* fault?" I asked.

She pursed her lips. Then shook her head no. "Talk to Pepper. This is one story I don't think I want to tell," Miss Bessie replied, uncharacteristically serious. "I should go find Gabe," she exhaled. "See if I can calm him down."

As she shuffled off slowly, I felt a new presence at my side.

Turning, I came face to face with Joe Arturo.

* * *

"Enjoying yourself?"

A wave of nausea hit me.

"That's a *strange* question to ask someone at a funeral reception, Mr. Arturo," I answered.

"It's strange to find the person charged with murdering my associate at the funeral reception of that same associate," Arturo countered mildly.

In fact, *everything* about the man was mild.

He was unremarkable. Not particularly handsome, not particularly ugly. Average. He wasn't tall; he wasn't short. He wasn't fat *or* thin. His suit wasn't expensive or well-fitting, but it wasn't Lester-level awkwardly sized, either. His eyes, his face were almost expressionless as he regarded me carefully while holding in his hand a Scotch on the rocks that seemed to be untouched.

Everything about Joe Arturo seemed fashioned to make him go unseen. He was a man easily overlooked...at least until you peered into his eyes.

"You and I both know that I was never charged with anything, Mr. Arturo," I told him politely, flinching under his fierce stare. I disliked his smugness intensely. At the very least, he was having an inappropriate relationship with Della Maddox, and that made him super sleazy. At the most, he was the murderer. "And I'm no longer accused of anything."

"Really?" he challenged me, his face cold. Lifeless. "That's not what I heard."

"Oh? What did you hear?"

"That the building inspector is trying to shut you down, ma'am," Joe answered with a half-grin. His eyes maintained their dead, cold examination of me, and I felt like prey under the gaze of a predator.

This was Lester's *great guy*?

How on earth did Lester *not* acknowledge this man's sociopathic energy? This was the guy that stepped in and was so *supportive*? Did *I* only sense it because I was a telepath?

The man made my skin crawl and my stomach churn with an intensity I had never felt before.

"That's right, your wife works in that department, doesn't she?" I asked, but he didn't respond. "Is she here? Your wife? I'd love to meet her," I said as I craned my neck to look among the crowd even though I had no idea who I was looking for.

"No, Carol stayed home," he responded after a protracted and uneasy silence. "She's taken ill recently," he continued with a self-satisfied smirk.

My head snapped back as I gawked at him.

Did he just basically imply he was making his wife sick? Like, right here? Out in the open? Something about what he said, something about the manner in which he said it...

I felt like I would throw up. I couldn't even name the feeling, it just...something reached in and clutched my guts in a vise.

He laughed at my discomfort, and it made my insides wither even further.

"Joe!" Della called, her expression unhappy to see the two of us together. "Come here!" He nodded to her and turned back to me.

"You know, it's a *shame* you did all that work to the building only to find yourself kicked out of it just a few months later," Joe said as he thrust his glass toward me. I felt cold liquid land on my chest. "I expect you could always sell that mutt back to Kane. Make him useful for something, since he ain't now."

"I would never sell Gideon," I hissed at the man, unable to even try to hide my disgust anymore. "He's a wonderful dog!"

Joe chuckled.

"Joe!" Della hollered more insistently.

"Coming!" he yelled back. Turning to me, he sneered. "At least Costco has a good return policy on those appliances," he told me, and then downed his drink in one gulp. "I suspect you won't be needing them soon."

Joe Arturo turned around and walked away.

SEVENTEEN

"Y ou're so *pale*, Fortuna," Pepper said as she made her way over to me and caught my hand. Her eyes widened when she realized it was shaking. "What happened?"

"*Visus*," Miss Bessie said as she followed us, her eyes wandering over my face. "It is the *knowing* that the mystic gets when face to face with wrong," the old woman confided as she leaned in to me.

"So anyone wrong, I can tell?" I asked her as the two of them escorted me to a bench on the edge of the patio. I felt unsteady, as if my legs had turned to jello.

Pepper's eyes lit up with excitement.

"Not *precisely*," Miss Bessie shook her head and

passed me water with lemon in it. "Drink, the water will help clear you."

"Then what is it, precisely?" Pepper asked the old woman.

"It's a sixth sense, a *knowing*, that something is not what it appears to be to everybody else. It's not mind reading, just...a sense. An understanding, a recognition that something, or someone, is not as it appears. The wider the divergence between what we see and what is real, the sharper the *visus*."

"And this just happens *randomly*?" I asked, alarmed.

"No, dear," Miss Bessie patted my hand. "You wouldn't be able to live an ordinary life if that were the case. People are wrong all the time. Nothing you saw would ever match up with anything anybody else saw. They would think you were a madwoman."

"It's because she was investigating the murder," Pepper guessed.

"Yes, dear," Bessie smiled at her.

"I can't block it?" I asked her, frowning. I had worked so hard to rein in my own supernatural powers so I could try to live in the mortal world without breaching the boundaries of everyone around me. That I suddenly had a new sense that was uncontrollable and that would also make me feel like I had the stomach flu was...distressing.

To put it mildly.

"It's just an *arrow*, dear, pointing you toward a path," Miss Bessie said as she pulled up a chair. "It doesn't tell you anything other than someone is not who they profess to be. I didn't think it would come on so strong, or I would have prepared you." She frowned, biting her lip. "Either you're quite strong, dear, or whoever you were talking to is *nothing* like they appear to be."

"Can I *force* this *visus* thing? Like, if I wanted to try it on someone?" I quizzed her.

Miss Bessie paused and shook her head no.

"Why not?" I asked.

"Because it's not a spell or a talent, dear," she told me rubbing my hand. "It's a *gift*, like a book."

"You can open a book when you want," I pointed out.

"Okay, it's like a television show that *shows* you what it wants you to see," Miss Bessie said, her smile dimming.

"You can stream a television—"

"It's a *broadcast* show," she grumbled, frowning. "From the *Fifties*. And it comes on when the company that owns the channel *wants* it on. Understand?"

"Fortuna, are you all right?" Lester asked as he stepped up to the three of us. The nerdy man's face fell, and his eyebrows knitted together. "Angie didn't pull something else, did she?"

"No, no, I'm fine, I'm just feeling a little faint, that's all," I told him as he kneeled down in front of me and reached into his pocket. His eyes showed concern. "Really, Lester I'm—"

"Let's just make sure, okay?" he smiled sympathetically. "I'm *not* a doctor, but I have one of our new wrist monitors with me." Lester pulled a black watch out of his pocket and placed it on my wrist, then pulled out his phone and tapped the screen. "Just breathe normally, I'll have the data here in a second."

I turned to look at the watch and saw the word *Spritetronic* in red across the face.

I felt my heart skip a beat.

"Whoa, your heart rate just zoomed a little there," Lester said as Pepper leaned forward to look at the watch, her eyes widening. "Maybe take some deep breaths, slow. That's it," he said as he nodded.

"*You* work for Spritetronic?" Pepper asked him, her eyes tightening.

"Yes, as a Senior Medical Device Engineer," Lester answered without looking up, his gaze still glued to the app's data on his screen. "This is one of our newest demos. I brought it with me so I could work on it when things...well, when I needed a diversion."

"Did you bring any *other* devices with you to work on?" Pepper asked. "Like...maybe the new wireless pacemaker monitor?"

Lester's eyes looked up at Pepper, and he frowned. "How did you know about that? The only place that's been written about is in trade journals."

"I know, I've read them," she informed him. "So, did you?"

He stood up and dropped the phone to his side, staring at her. Confusion clouded his expression. "Yes, three," he responded haltingly. His eyes narrowed. "Why are you asking me this, Pepper?"

"Do you still have *all* three?" she asked him without explaining anything to him.

His frown intensified. "Of course I do. They're upstairs in my room."

"You're staying here?" I asked, surprised.

"We both did, to help prepare for the party," Lester said as he looked down at me. "Me, my father. The house is huge, so we always stay in the east wing for a week around the party to help out, spend time with the family."

"Show me," Pepper told him.

Lester stared at her for a moment. I could tell that he wanted to ask more questions, and he was *clearly* concerned about the turn the conversation had taken—but in the end, he just nodded and gestured for us to follow him.

Pepper, Miss Bessie and I followed Lester back into the house.

None of us noticed someone observing us.

Our ears never burned to indicate someone was listening to us.

And we definitely didn't realize we were being followed.

* * *

"It *has* to be here," Lester muttered as he frantically dumped out his satchel and flung clothing in all directions. "Do any of you see it?" he asked, looking up, his eyes wide. "It's a small black disk, about yay big," he said as he circled his fingers to show a half-dollar sized space.

"Looks like these two, right?" Pepper pointed to the two disks on the desk.

"Yeah, it...I don't understand."

"I think I do," Pepper replied, nodding.

"Hold on a second, Pepper," I told her, and then turned to Lester. "Why did you bring them here? Same thing as the watch, just to work on them?"

"Yeah. Well, no...not entirely," he clarified as he sat down, disheartened, on the lavish bed. "Uncle Hugh has a Spritetronic pacemaker. Because of his age, they—his doctors—had the heart rate set pretty low. Too low for him and his...um, more strenuous activities?" Lester told us, blushing somewhat.

"You can change that for him, though," I suggested. Lester nodded.

"Someone from the company has to do it with a special code, and I checked—it wasn't dangerous or anything. It was just a huge pain in the backside for him to go to the doctor, get the code changed, and his pacemaker? It had a failsafe reset so every week or so, it would go back to what it used to be."

"Your solution?"

Lester shifted uncomfortably. Finally, he sighed. "I gave him a computer and the software so he could change it himself about a year ago. I thought I could assess the wireless product while I was here on a real, implanted pacemaker."

Miss Bessie's mouth gaped open.

"Don't look at me like that!" Lester told her, wincing under Miss Bessie's silent scrutiny. "It's not dangerous, and as far as the pacemaker settings, I made sure he couldn't change it outside of certain specifications. He could only do particular things in the settings that were safe. And he helped me pay for school...I owed him."

"You don't owe family," Miss Bessie rolled her eyes.

"So he couldn't have, say, set up the pacemaker

to shoot off the defibrillator at the wrong time?" Pepper asked.

"Absolutely not!" Lester's expression was horrified. "To change the software outside of certain parameters, you'd need an admin override code. He did *not* have that. I never would have given him that."

"You mean *that* admin override code?" I asked, pointing to a paper laying on the desk. Someone had written a long string of letters and numbers on it. In parentheses it said: PM Override Model #DD47286-ST.

Lester stared, his face turning white.

"So, here's the thing," Pepper told him as she put her hands on her hips. "Your missing disk thing is back at Fortuna's shop. I got it from the orchid on Hugh's lapel. The one he was wearing the night he was killed."

Lester blinked rapidly, his chest rising and falling with shallow, panicked breaths.

"Did you talk to anyone about all this?" I asked him. "The code, the disk?"

"Well, my uncle!" he choked. "Obviously, *he* knew."

"Anyone sitting next to him while you spoke to him about it?"

Lester looked away, tears springing to his eyes.

"Come on, Lester, *who* overheard you talk about this with him?" Pepper pressed.

He shook his head no. "It's *not* possible. It couldn't be."

"What's not possible?" I asked him.

Miss Bessie stared, calmly, her shoulders tense. "Just tell them, child," she declared as Lester seemed to collapse in on himself.

"I don't think so," Joe Arturo said as he slithered into the room, a gun pointed straight at Lester.

* * *

"I t was *you* that planted the paint, wasn't it?" I challenged him as he arranged each of us in a particular place in the room. Arturo waved us this way and that way, as if he was staging a scene. "How *else* would you know I shop at Costco?"

"It would have been more advantageous to me if you'd just gone down for it," Joe replied as he calmly positioned Miss Bessie on the floor face down. Turning to Pepper, he twisted her down next to Miss Bessie beside him. "I knew the paint would be the nail in your coffin, and the police wouldn't bother to look beyond that once they found it. I *didn't* count on them being too stupid to find it."

"But you volunteered to pretend to test the paint just to be sure?"

"*That* was just a happy accident," Joe Arturo smiled. "A sign of the divine blessing for what I'd done, I expect." He picked Lester up roughly and thrust him toward me. Hugh's nephew stood to my right as we gazed at the polished black gun across the room.

The sleazeball waved it like a toy as it punctuated his words, and my breath caught every moment its aim whizzed toward my head. It was evident from the fact that Joe had split us up all around the room and the way he handled his pistol he wasn't experienced in military strategy or firearms, so that was *something*.

But...there was still nowhere to go, and his lack of expertise made the whole situation seem even more dangerous.

If I ran out the door, he could squeeze a bullet off before I got halfway there even *without* training. We weren't that far apart, and he had a clear shot. Even if I could make it out to get Gabe for help—I mean, I couldn't leave everyone in this room with an armed crazy person.

Think, Fortuna, think.

"Why?" Lester asked, the words choked out as if they were painful to say. "My uncle's always been good to you. You were *his friend*—"

"No!" Joe shouted and walked up to Lester. "Hugh Maddox was an awful friend! He gave me the rejects, made me dance for every investment I ever got, every favor he ever did me! And he treated Della like she was rubbish!"

The last statement rang of truth, and of something...*hidden*. My gut churned with what might have been Bessie's *visus*...or might have been fear of death.

One or the other.

"You *truly* love Della, don't you?" I inquired tenderly as I impulsively tugged down layer after layer of mental self-containment and reached out into Joe Arturo's mind. Ethics be damned—this guy had a gun on us.

If *he* could hold me at gunpoint, *I* could rummage through his brain like it was a junk drawer.

He studied me, his expression confused by my manner, and he concentrated on me attentively. With that intense focus connecting us, I slid right in —and I confirmed what I think everyone in the room already recognized.

He had no intention of letting anybody out of here alive.

"She's Hugh's widow," Joe replied warily, his eyes locked on mine.

"That's what she is, not how you feel about her," I explained to him, my voice soothing as his face grew contorted. "You really love her, don't you?" I repeated. Pepper slowly lifted her head up and glanced around the room while Joe focused his undivided attention on me.

"I love her," Arturo said in a bleak, rasping tone, as if the words were painful to say.

"And that's why you killed Hugh for her?" I suggested.

"No, no, that's not what happened," Lester answered, tossing his head back and forth as if trying to evade the awareness in his mind. "It *couldn't* have just been him. He wasn't in this house at all, not at *all*, before they executed my uncle." Lester's eyes were glued to his uncle's friend.

"You shut your mouth, boy," Joe Arturo warned.

Neither of them noticed Pepper move her body an inch closer to Joe.

"My Aunt Della...she...she..." Lester was overcome with rage and sadness.

"She tired of your uncle running around and bedding every loose woman, trollop, and tart from here to the Arkansas River, son," Joe sneered at the weeping man. "And so she came in here, got the code, and taught me what needed to be done to free her. To free us all from—"

"Oh my god, you're going to murder us, aren't you?" Pepper shrieked in a panic, wrapping her fists around Joe Arturo's leg. She had dragged herself inch by inch toward him until she had covered the foot and a half between them, gotten so close that she could use his body to pull herself to her knees as she begged him for her life.

Which she did.

"Get off me!" Joe turned on her and struggled to weaken her hold on his leg, but she was like a hysterical octopus with a vise grip. He held the gun pointed toward the window as he endeavored to peel Pepper off him.

"Why else would you confess!" Pepper screeched. "You're going to kill us! You're going to kill us all!" The two of them struggled, Pepper to clutch him tightly and Joe Arturo to get the wailing woman back on the floor.

The diversion gave Gabe just enough time to vault into the suite from the corridor, smash Joe Arturo on the head and shove him against the wall.

"You're under arrest," Gabe said as he disarmed the dazed man.

"It was just me!" he snarled. "It wasn't Della! Just me, Wilcox, just me!"

"It *was Della*," Lester said furiously as he rubbed the tears from his face. He strode over to his laptop resting on the desk, plugged in a USB drive, and moved his finger around briskly. Yanking it out with a flourish, he swung toward Gabe and handed it to him. "This should put *that* man *and* my aunt away for killing my uncle. He spilled the whole thing, and it's on video."

Joe's shoulders slumped as Gabe took the drive and nodded.

"Before we get to inventorying the crime scene, could someone help me up off the *damn floor?*" Miss Bessie asked as she struggled to push herself to her hands and knees.

Pepper and I jumped to help the old woman as Gabe called for backup.

EIGHTEEN

G abe had rushed us out of Lester's room pretty quickly, and additional officers arrived just as we descended the main staircase. It didn't take long for the crowd outside to come in to see what the hubbub was about.

"Joe, *what* is going on?" Della asked as she stamped her high-heeled foot with all the pretension of a monarch. When Joe paid no mind to her, his head sagged to his chest, she whirled on Gabe and demanded an explanation. "Detective, *what* is the purpose of this?"

If it worried her, nothing in her face showed it.

"Can you take him?" Gabe said to a youthful officer dazzled by the affluence and opulence of the Maddoxes' mansion. Pulling his gaze from the art on the walls, Officer Smith nodded hastily and grasped the shackled, dazed Joe Arturo. As the young cop turned, Gabe pulled the handcuffs dangling from his belt and angled toward Della.

"Della Maddox, you're under arrest for the murder of Hugh Maddox."

The crowd gasped and drew away from Della in one sudden movement. She stopped, annoyed, in the center of the foyer staring at Gabe as if she heard—and dismissed— his accusation before he finished speaking it.

"That's preposterous," she scoffed, her eyes narrowing. "That woman," she howled as she raised her arm to point at me, "electrocuted my poor Hugh! If we should arrest anybody, it should be her!"

"I know what you did," Lester said as he stepped out from behind Pepper. "I know what you did, I know how you did it, and I—"

"Bob," Della called behind her as Gabe continued to progress. "Come here and get your *fairy* son under control! Your boy—if you can even *call* him that—has lost his mind!" Her face distorted with contempt as she mocked her nephew.

I gasped.

"Murdering bigot," Lester whispered.

"Deviant sissy," she spat back as Gabe spun her

around a little more roughly than called for and placed her in the handcuffs.

"What's going on?" Bob Maddox asked as he shoved to the front of the collected crowd. His head twisted this way and that way as he took in Gabe handcuffing Della, the two uniformed officers assisting him, and the crestfallen face of his only child. "Lester, what happened?"

"Dad, she *murdered* him," Lester told his father, the grief shining through his words. "Della and Joe Arturo. They killed Uncle Hugh."

"No, it's not possible...She...Della, is this true?" Bob asked his sister-in-law, his eyes swelling with tears as the color drained from his face.

"Of course it's not true, you moron!"

Lester seethed at her denial. "Joe *told* us she did it when he was trying to kill us—"

"Trying to *what*?" Bob whirled toward his son and shot over. Frantically examining him, he asked, "Are you all right? Are you hurt?"

"No, Dad, I'm fine. Physically, anyhow," he scowled at Della.

"You killed Hugh!" Della protested as Gabe led her toward the door. "You did it so you could get Hugh's wealth for your father, you pansy! It was your program that did it! *Your* software that induced his heart attack!"

Did she really...she didn't just blurt out the modus operandi, did she?

"Hey, Della?" Pepper called.

"What?"

"How did you suddenly realize that it was Lester's software that caused your husband's heart attack?" Pepper asked as she crossed her arms. "Didn't you just say Fortuna did it, like, *two* minutes ago?"

"Well, he just said—"

"Lester told his father you murdered your husband," she said, cutting the bound woman off. "No one said a single thing about how Lester thought you did it. But way to go for confirming." Pepper smiled fiercely at the woman. "That should make prosecuting you a lot easier, I would think."

"I...but I..." Della seemed astonished that she had made such a rookie mistake.

"You never knew when to keep your lip *zipped*, Della," Miss Bessie muttered. Della glared at her with daggers as another officer led her out to join her co-conspirator.

If the police in this town were a little wanting in the intelligence department, it seemed the offenders were a few burgers short of a barbecue themselves. Though maybe that wasn't quite a fair assessment—

they almost framed me for it. I glanced at Pepper with an elevated respect for her ability to sniff out a mystery no one else could see.

Without her initial digging, I *might* have gotten snagged in their trap.

* * *

"Fortuna! Fortuna, are you all right?" I pivoted around to spot a stricken Martin Salvi headed toward me, his driver Jeeves trailing him for the first time that afternoon. Jeeves—real name Chris—studied the surroundings like a shark searching for chum in the water.

"I'm fine," I nodded as he embraced me. He held me so tight that my cheek squished against Martin's rock-solid, muscled chest. His hand curled up my back and pressed my head into his body so hard I worried I might suffocate. His pulse was so fast...

"I was so concerned," he murmured, shaken. "*Thank God* you're all right." His grasp loosened somewhat, but he didn't let me go.

"It wasn't God, really," I said as I tugged away lightly and peeked up. "It was Gabriel. Well, Gabriel *and* Pepper, I presume," I explained as I twisted toward Pepper. "That whole *please don't kill me* thing, that was just a diversion, wasn't it?"

"I saw Gabe in the corridor," Pepper nodded as the three of us stepped toward the side of the room. "Shooting Joe from there would have been risky, so I tried to hold his attention to give Gabe a better shot at saving us."

"You did at that. That was amazing," I told her as I watched Gabe talk to the officers through the bay window. "Both of you."

"You were pretty good yourself," she told me, but I shook my head no. "Oh, come on, Fortuna, you mean to tell me you weren't—"

"I just stood there and waited to be rescued," I countered, staring at her, my eyes wide as I tried to remind Pepper with a look that Martin knew nothing of my paranormal abilities.

Pepper glanced at Martin and nodded, turning toward the window to watch Gabe, too.

"He will be unbearable now, the hero Wilcox," Pepper said with a smirk. "His head will be bigger than a hot-air balloon."

"No. It won't," Miss Bessie said as she walked up, her eyes glued to Pepper's face. She turned and faced the old woman's gaze. They looked at one another until the younger woman fidgeted restlessly and looked away. "My Gabriel wouldn't let this affect him at all. And you know it."

Out the window I could see Liz, my friend and neighbor from the hair salon next door to my shop, arriving with Claire, Miss Bessie's caretaker. Gabe must have called them to take care of Miss Bessie since, now, Gabe had to run a crime scene. I felt a little hurt that he didn't ask me to take Miss Bessie home, and then I understood why he wouldn't have —I arrived with Martin.

Whatever this was between them? It was galling.

"Will you pardon me for a moment?" Martin inquired, and I nodded. He looked reluctant to let his hands drop, and he leaned in one more time for another brief hug. "I'm so glad you're all right. I don't know what I would do if...anyway, I'll be back in a moment. There's something I have to do."

As I watched him walk away, Pepper leaned in to me and murmured, "That guy? That guy's in love with you."

"Oh, my *mercy*, don't be absurd," I told her, chuckling. "Whatever he heard about what happened upstairs was probably a thousand times worse than what really happened, that's all. He's just rattled, I'd guess."

"You know, if you did more than guess, you might realize that guy has some deep feelings for you," Pepper replied.

"I will not dig around in his brain."

"Well, then might I suggest just opening your eyes?"

"Pepper, stop," I said as Liz and Claire made their way over to us. "You're being ridiculous. We barely know one another."

"What on earth happened?" Liz asked as Claire moved in beside Miss Bessie and planted her hand on the old woman's elbow lightly. "Gabe called Claire and said you guys were involved in some kind of shooting?"

"No one got shot, thanks to Pepper," I responded.

"No, it was really thanks to Gabe," Pepper said, waving away the credit for her Oscar winning performance.

"It looks like Martin thinks that, too," Miss Bessie said as she pointed out the window where the two men, Martin and Gabe, stood across from one another talking.

"Oh, no," I murmured.

"Oh, dear," Liz added.

"Wow, you two have no faith in *anyone*, do you?" Pepper said. I looked at her and then spun back to watch Gabriel and Martin standing on the driveway alone.

We all stared quietly.

A moment later, Martin presented his hand to Gabe and waited.

"Do you think he'll do it?" Liz asked.

"Why wouldn't he?" I responded.

"They have a history," Pepper said.

"They'll be fine," Miss Bessie added.

Claire said nothing, and Miss Bessie stared at her impatiently.

"I'm on the clock, it doesn't seem right to make a personal observation when Gabe pays me," Claire told her primly. Miss Bessie rolled her eyes.

Gabe slowly extended his hand, and the two men shook.

Pepper smiled proudly. "I knew he would."

"And Martin left Jeeves here," Liz said as she pointed to the driver standing five feet from our group. He continued scanning the area silently, like a robot. "*That* was a show of trust, Martin going out there alone."

"Martin went around the place all day without Jeeves," I told Liz. "I wouldn't read all that much into it."

"What *I* read is that he values *you* more than his own life," Pepper told me. I blushed. "I'm telling you, Delphi, that man's got it hot and heavy for you. Maybe it's time to stop toying with him and push your relationship forward to after-dinner drinks?"

"Okay, *enough*, Pepper."

"She'll kick herself when she lets him get away," Liz laughed.

"Are you kidding?" Pepper scoffed as she eyed

Jeeves again. "That guy? That guy's not going *anywhere*."

To my surprise, Miss Bessie did not comment again that I was intended for her grandson, Gabriel. In fact, she peered back and forth between Pepper and Gabe again, her face lined with apprehension.

* * *

"Gerard called while you were upstairs," Martin spoke as we sat side by side in the back of his limo. The privacy partition was up, but I could vaguely hear the radio station Jeeves was listening to. "The papers they served you with were not, strictly speaking, legitimate. The eviction issue has been taken care of as he promised."

"Someone faked the papers?"

"Oh, they were real all right," Martin said as he shifted toward me. "They had been filed properly, and there would have been a hearing. But Carol Arturo didn't file them even though her signature was on them."

I frowned. "Who did?"

"Gabe will look into it, but since Carol is in the hospital with arsenic poisoning, I will venture a guess and say that Joe slipped the papers in with an envelope of things his wife worked on while ill," he told me as I gasped, horrified. "I think he saw the opportunity to continue to shift the focus, and so he did."

"Arsenic poisoning? Is Carol going to be okay?"

"The doctors think so. She's apparently a little shaken. And a lot angry. She has an exceptional attorney, however," Martin smiled. "He should be able to help her detach herself from that horrible human being."

"I guess they think Joe poisoned his wife?"

"That's Gerard's guess, yes," Martin responded. "Gerard was with Carol in her hospital room when she got the call that they arrested her husband. The two of them put the pieces together. I don't know that the police have looked into it yet, but I'm sure Gabe will."

"So, it's *Gabe* now, huh?" I asked with a half-smirk.

Martin returned my look with a resolute gaze, his face an unreadable mask. After a few moments, he took a sharp breath. "I owed him for keeping you safe."

"You know, he kept Miss Bessie, Pepper, and Lester safe, too."

"I owed him for keeping you safe," Martin echoed once again with no change in his expression or tone. Not a flicker of emotion. The air in the limo seemed to chill.

.   .   .

I frowned.

Martin was...hiding something.

No, not *hiding* something. Pretending something wasn't the way it was, or putting on a front so I wouldn't pick up on something.

There were moments with him where I knew, I sensed, he wasn't *quite* being real with me. It had nothing to do with telepathy, or *visus*, or anything magical.

It was just me, a girl, knowing that he, a boy, wasn't being *entirely* honest.

I studied him but his face, his eyes, gave away nothing.

Back at the mansion, Martin was spontaneous and expressive and agitated about what I went through. I could see it. Frustrated at feeling powerless, maybe. He enclosed me in his arms with no concern for crossing lines, breaking rules. He held me because he *needed* to.

Now, he seemed untouched by what I'd been through.

Now, he looked to need *nothing*.

"You are a *very* complicated man, Mr. Salvi," I confided as I reached out to grab his hand in an effort to thaw whatever freeze had just occurred. His hand was cool, and soft, and when I squeezed it, it was...passive in response. He didn't squeeze back. "Thank you for being my friend," I tried once more.

"Of course," he informed me. No warmth. No tenderness. No friendliness.

Distance.

He pulled his hand away gently, placed it in his lap and glanced out the window.

I scrutinized him struggling to figure out *what* had just taken place.

NINETEEN

"That's fantastic," I told Azalea as I looked at her oil painting. "The colors you used are just so delicate." The seventeen-year-old had painted the angel I had created based on the sketches she made the day this craziness started. It was a huge canvas, and the angel practically gleamed.

"Can you see who's in the fog behind it?" she asked me excitedly.

Squinting, I realized she had done a wispy, ethereal shadow of the late Hugh Maddox. "Oh, Azalea, that's very—"

"I will give it to Mr. Maddox," the young woman nodded, excitedly cutting me off. Her pixie-like nose was smeared with baby blue paint. "Everyone forgets that statue was for his dad, you know? I thought he'd like something that memorialized his brother in a happier way."

"I think he'll like it very much," I told her.

Or, you know, it would haunt him for the rest of his life. One of the two.

Gideon began barking just as the chimes from the front door reached me. "I'll be right back, Azalea," I told her. She nodded, not taking her critical eyes off her own work as she dabbed here and frowned there.

"Lester?" I said, surprised to find Bob's son in my shop. "Is everything okay?"

"Yes, everything's fine," he said, sniffling, as his eyes wandered over the walls and the art displayed there. "Did you do all these?"

"Most of them," I told him, nodding. "As I get more students, I'm slowly replacing my work with theirs. I'd love for the gallery to eventually show a real variety of mediums and styles."

"You have a distinct style, don't you?" Lester smiled as he pointed toward the large self-portrait.

"How are you doing?" I asked him as I handed him a cup of tea. He accepted it gratefully, and I gestured toward the seating area.

"I feel like I've been stuck in a maelstrom,

really," he admitted, pausing to take a sip of the hot tea. "Dad's overwhelmed. He always knew he was the second son, you know? So it never occurred to him he would inherit Granddad's fortune, or the businesses."

"It's only been four days, and there's been no trial—how did it all happen so fast?" I asked him.

"There won't be a trial," Lester told me leaning back. "Between the security footage from my room, Joe turning on Aunt Della, and what she said in front of everybody? She knew she was toast. They both cut a deal to keep the death penalty off the table within hours of being interrogated."

"The prosecutor was going to try to seek the death penalty?" I asked, startled.

"Pecuniary gain is a qualifier," he answered.

"What's that?"

"Killing someone for money."

"Well, I guess there's no argument that they did that," I said, tilting my head. "Have you heard anything about Carol Arturo? Martin told me it seemed like Joe was trying to poison her?"

"It seemed like it because he was. I saw her yesterday," Lester nodded. "She's recovering pretty well, all things considered. Dad and I wanted to make sure we took care of her hospital bills."

"That's very kind of you."

"It was the right thing to do," Lester countered. "We have access to Della's money—well, I guess it's Dad's money now—and since Della caused all this, Dad felt Carol was owed that, at least."

"So it was Della's idea to murder your uncle? Not Joe's?"

"Oh, I think Joe had built up a head of steam over the years about Uncle Hugh," Lester mused as he gazed at a painting. "He was never as successful as my uncle, but never seemed to realize that was just an accident of birth. He resented that Uncle Hugh seemed to always have everything, get away with everything. I think Della, once she got fed up, realized she could manipulate him. And so she did."

"That's so awful for your family," I told Lester.

"Well, it's just me and Dad now. Ed's my family," he smiled.

"Are you staying in town much longer?" I asked him.

He shook his head no.

"That's why I wanted to stop by," Lester said as he leaned forward and placed his cup on the coffee table. "I ran into Pepper and said this to her, but I wanted to say it to you, too. Thank you."

"Thank *me*?" I asked him, surprised. "For what?"

"You and Pepper seemed to be the only people

that knew there was something else going on," he admitted. "I realize you wound up involved in this because they framed you, but once they didn't find the paint Joe planted and you had lawyers handling the paperwork thing with the building code, you could have just let it go. You didn't."

"Oh, Lester, I'm sure the building code thing would have exposed what was going on. My lawyer was meeting with Carol Arturo—"

"While Joe Arturo was holding a gun on us," Lester pointed out. "If I didn't know about any of that, I could have said the wrong thing to the wrong person about the security video I had of my room, and someone could have decided to take me out because of it. You know, I had a video of Uncle Hugh."

"You did?"

"Yes," he nodded. "From the day he died. I had been planning to share it with Aunt Della after the funeral. If I innocently told her I kept the cam on all the time, not knowing..." Lester trailed off, his mouth dropping into a troubled frown. "Well, things could have ended differently for me."

"Why *do* you keep your laptop recording video all the time?" I asked him. It had nailed the case against Joe and Della, but that Lester did it at all had me curious.

"Work habit," he told me, shrugging. "It records work that I do and I...uh, I talk to myself," Lester smiled sheepishly. "Sometimes, I don't remember what I said or my own observations as I'm working out issues. Leaving it running all the time just became easier, and I can toss out whatever I don't need later or reference what I do need."

That made sense. And was actually a fantastic idea. I contemplated installing video cameras in the studio so people could watch themselves create—

"In any case, you and Pepper helped to uncover what happened so quickly, and no one—other than Uncle Hugh—got hurt," he told me, smiling. "So, thank you."

"Anytime," I smiled.

* * *

"Finally!" Pepper said as she waved the newspaper at me.

"Finally, what?" I asked as I looked up from a rather boring bowl of chicken soup. Spike hovered around Pepper trying to read the front page as she whirled it around while Gideon jumped at it, barking.

"Oh, no, pup, you will not eat this copy," Pepper told me as she sat down at my kitchen counter across from me and eyed my canned soup. "Well, *we've* certainly fallen far away from shrimp scampi."

I winced slightly at Pepper's reminder that Martin Salvi had not called me or dropped by since the day of the two arrests at the Maddox mansion. On the third day, I tried to reach out to him but my calls only went to voice mail.

"Don't remind me," I told her. "Tell me, what's with the paper?"

"A front page byline," she crowed proudly as she held the paper up with two hands in front of her. "A real, honest-to-goodness news story about the murder and the subsequent shenanigans."

"You mean like being held at gunpoint?" I asked her. "*Those* shenanigans?"

"Shenanigans is a *very* versatile word," Pepper told me seriously.

"Congratulations, Pepper. I'm thrilled for you."

Pepper lowered the paper to the counter and stared at me, gesturing toward my soup. "He really hasn't called? Nothing?"

I shook my head no.

"Have you talked to Gabe about it?"

"Why would I talk to Gabe about it?"

"He seemed to be the last conversation Martin had before he went ice cold on you," Pepper said as she pulled out her phone and tapped the screen. "Did he tell you what they said to each other? Because he didn't tell me."

"Pepper, stop," I said as I lurched forward and tried to grab her phone, but she jumped up from the stool and walked toward the living room.

"Gabe? We need you over at Fortuna's," Pepper said as she walked around the room while I tried to catch her. "No, tomorrow at 3 p.m. for an art contest judging. Of course right now. If I *wanted* you to come later? I would have *called* you later." Another pause. "You can ignore a text, that's why. See you soon."

"You are the most *infuriating* human being I have ever met," I told her, crossing my arms.

"Hard to believe," she told me. "I mean, you lived in California, for goodness' sake."

* * *

"What's wrong?" Gabe asked me as he came in, badge hanging off his belt and hand resting lightly on his gun. His eyes swept the room looking for threats.

"I want it noted for the record that I did not call you here," I told him. "Nothing's wrong, she's—"

"Why hasn't Martin called her in *four days*?" Pepper asked Gabe. While she didn't make a wholesale accusation that Martin's lack of communication was somehow Gabe's fault, there seemed to be an intimation to her remarks that Martin's lack of communication was somehow Gabe's fault.

Gabe hesitated, dropped his hands, and gawked at Pepper.

"Well?" she pressed.

"Did you *honestly* call me in the middle of dinner and have me *drop everything* to rush over here and answer *your* questions about *Fortuna's love life?*" Gabe asked Pepper.

"She's in *pain,*" Pepper pointed to me.

"I'm not in pain," I told Gabriel.

"You are *incredible,*" Gabe told Pepper.

"And you spoke to the man that had been fastened to Fortuna like bubblegum in hair. Then, abruptly, he won't talk to her anymore," Pepper pointed out, her eyes narrowing. "I wouldn't think you'd kneecap the competition, Gabe, but—"

"Competition for what?" Gabe asked, his eyes wide.

"Her, plainly," Pepper pointed at me.

"Hey, guys, I'm *right* here." I waved. It was as if neither one of them saw me or remembered I was in the room as a real, living, breathing being. I seemed like a minor prop in another one of their quarrels.

Gideon sat between them glancing back and

forth. Then the dog produced a noise that sounded suspiciously like *Huh?*

"She's a *friend*, Pepper," Gabe told her with a fierce glare. I could practically feel the adrenaline coursing through his body. It was feeding an irritation that he looked to be having trouble managing. "Even if she wasn't, it would be no business of yours. That was your decision. *Remember?*"

"This isn't about *us*—"

"*Isn't* it?"

I don't know *why* Miss Bessie thought Gabe and I would wind up together. Gabriel Wilcox and Pepper Stanford were so fixed into one another I could almost see a silver cord between the two of them. Aside from a few flickers of attraction from Gabe, he had never given me *any* sign he wanted to be more than friends.

"Why did you two break up?" I asked in as tranquil a voice as I could muster.

"You don't have to use that *soothe the hysterical person* tone, Fortuna, I don't think he'll shoot me," Pepper replied as her eyes stayed glued to her former love's face. "No matter how much he may prefer to."

"We broke up because she—"

"Gabe, it doesn't matter—"

"—takes risks that will get her *killed*," Gabe

finished. "And she doesn't want to put me through that again."

"That's not why—"

"It *is* why!" Gabe shouted at her, his hands balling into fists. "You would rather be alone and take risks than be with me and let me look after you! You left me because I cared—"

"I left you because you tried to *manage* me," Pepper choked out, her eyes somewhat red-rimmed. "I needed to live my life, Gabe. My life, making my own decisions. You wouldn't let me do that—"

"Ironic, considering Martin cut *her* off for the exact opposite reason," Gabe told Pepper as he glanced away from her, his eyes landing on me. "Pepper left me because I worked to persuade her to be more vigilant. Martin left you because the idea of you being hurt or murdered was so stunning to him, *he* couldn't take it."

"I don't understand," I frowned.

"No, neither of you do! *She* left because she didn't want me to *worry*," Gabe said, pointing at Pepper. "She wouldn't change, and she didn't want me to worry. Martin left because *he* didn't want to worry or put *you* at risk or try to control you."

"Put me at risk for *what*?" I asked him.

"Oh, Gabe," Pepper whispered as she brushed a lone tear aside.

"You know what? Forget it. You're both going to

do whatever you want," Gabe said as he spun on his heel and made his way toward the stairs. "I know that. I get it. You've consistently been that way, Pepper. Fortuna, you've clearly joined her in whatever crusade she's on. Neither of you will accept advice from anyone."

Gabriel paused at the top of the stairs and shifted to study both of us. "But this is a *nasty* town. One with *secrets*. Secret agendas," he declared. "If you two plan to make it your mission to charge headlong into that danger again and again, that's your choice. You've been lucky so far, I'll grant you that. One day? One day that luck will run *out*."

Gabe ran down the stairs as I remained, dumbstruck, struggling to understand—again—what had just happened.

Spike and Gideon looked at us silently.

"*Now* do you understand why there are so many lesbians in this town?" Pepper asked as she sighed and sat down on the bench. A tendon in her jaw twitched as her expression hardened. "I think it's an evolutionary defense. The men in this town. I swear."

I wasn't sure I understood anything about Mystic's End.

But if I would remain here, I apparently needed to work a little harder to figure it out.

THANK YOU FOR READING!

I hope you enjoyed Angel in Demise! Please think about leaving a review! Fortuna and Gideon's adventures continue in Book 3, Sketchy Charms!

KEEP UP WITH LEANNE LEEDS

Thanks so much for reading! I hope you liked it! Want to keep up with me?

Visit leanneleeds.com to:

Find all my books...

Sign up for my newsletter...

Like me on Facebook...

Follow me on Twitter...

Follow me on Instagram...

Thanks again for reading!

Leanne Leeds

FIND A TYPO? LET US KNOW!

Typos happen. It's sad, but true.

Though we go over the manuscript multiple times, have editors, have beta readers, and advance readers it's inevitable that determined typos and mistakes sometimes find their way into a published book.

Did you find one? If you did, think about reporting it on leanneleeds.com so we can get it corrected.

www.ingramcontent.com/pod-product-compliance
Lightning Source LLC
Chambersburg PA
CBHW031938240626
47153CB00003B/782